Other Novels by Mildred Walker
Available in Bison Books Editions

Unless the Wind Turns

Mildred Walker

Introduction to the Bison Books Edition
by Deirdre McNamer

UNIVERSITY OF NEBRASKA PRESS
LINCOLN AND LONDON

♾ The paper in this book meets the minimum requirements of
American National Standard for Information Sciences—Perma-
nence of Paper for Printed Library Materials, ANSI Z39.48-1984.

First Bison Books printing: 1996
Most recent printing indicated by the last digit below:
10   9   8   7   6   5   4   3   2   1

Library of Congress Cataloging-in-Publication Data
Walker, Mildred, 1905–
Unless the wind turns / Mildred Walker; introduction by Deirdre
McNamer.
p.   cm.
ISBN 0-8032-9781-5 (pbk.: alk. paper)
I. Title.
PS3545.A524U5   1996
813'.54—dc20
96-780   CIP

Reprinted from the original 1941 edition by Harcourt, Brace and
Company, New York.

PORTIA

Within the bond of marriage, tell me, Brutus,
Is it excepted I should know no secrets
That appertain to you? Am I yourself
But, as it were, in sort or limitation,
To keep with you at meals, comfort your bed,
And talk to you sometimes? Dwell I
     but in the suburbs
Of your good pleasure? If it be no more,
Portia is Brutus' harlot, not his wife.

BRUTUS

. . . Portia, go in a while;
And by and by thy bosom shall partake
The secrets of my heart.

Julius Caesar
ACT II, Scene i

INTRODUCTION

Deirdre McNamer

When Mildred Walker began to write *Unless the Wind Turns*, her fifth novel, the Depression was drawing to a close and the world was on the brink of its second multinational conflagration. All the shapes were shifting.

Walker, born in 1905, had grown up in Pennsylvania and Vermont, a bright and well-educated daughter of a parson and a schoolteacher. Now she lived in a windy little city called Great Falls, out on the Montana plains about thirty miles east of the Rocky Mountains. Her husband practiced medicine. They hadn't lived long in the West. Walker was in her mid-thirties, had three young children and seemed on the verge of a national literary reputation. Her previous book, *Dr. Norton's Wife*, had been the January 1939 selection of the Literary Guild of America, which called her "a master of the novel form" and exuberantly predicted that she was about to move out of undeserved obscurity to become "one of the American writers of front rank importance."

It could be said that Walker, at this point, occupied the kinds of borderlands—historical, professional, and social—that encourage unease. America was on the border of war. She herself seemed to be on the border of fame. And, in her daily life, she regularly traversed the border between her public and private realms. To Great Falls, she was Mrs. Ferdinand Schemm, the conventional and spirited doctor's wife. (In college, she was known as "Pep" Walker.) She worked energetically to achieve the right ambience and amenities in her home; the right manners in her children; the kinds of dinner parties and teas at which she could shine.

At the same time, she was Mildred Walker, the writer, who worked steadily and fervently at her solitary occupation with virtually no encouragement or literary cameraderie except that provided by her remarkable husband, who took her efforts as seriously as she did. The household was run by hired help, so she could write. When each book was finished, she asked her husband to read it, and no one else, and then it was sent to her publisher.

The far eastern edge of the Rockies, where *Unless the Wind Turns* is set, is itself a kind of border region between the shadowy mountains and the tawny flatness of the nearby plains. Those of us who are familiar with that corridor know the ways in which it can be at once gorgeous and daunting; exhilarating and depleting. The wind blows very hard. Summer is brief. Out on the plains, there is the sense among some of us, at some times, of being cast off from land and shelter—the land being the Rockies—onto a grand and treeless sea that undulates to its own rhythms and weather, its few humans floating like specks on the broad water.

None of this was lost on Walker. Like most fine novelists, she seemed interested in places and people (perhaps including herself) that are sometimes one thing, sometimes another. She exhibited, early on, an interest in ambivalence and a tolerance for it.

All this is by way of suggesting that *Unless the Wind Turns*, the first novel in which Walker placed her characters in the West, is a study in the ways that characters and places can seem to contain their own opposites.

The book interweaves several stories: the story of a troubled marriage; an exploration of easterners versus westerners; and a pure adventure—a few men trying to fight, then to escape, a thunderous forest fire. (Walker no doubt drew on a large fire that had swept through a drainage of the Teton River in 1938, not far from where the Schemms had a cabin. The tragic Mann Gulch fire that Norman Maclean immortalized in *Young Men and Fire* broke out further east in Montana in 1949.)

When the novel opens, we meet John Davis, who spent part of his boyhood in a Montana town on the prairie east of the mountains. He has brought his eastern-born-and-bred wife, Serena, to the Montana mountains for a horseback vacation that he hopes will revive their flagging affections. She, however, has invited others along: her friend Lizzie and Lizzie's physician husband Walt, and another physician named Victor, a refugee from Nazi Germany whom Serena has befriended and is attracted to. John and Serena are not, as we would say today, communicating well.

John is the only westerner in the bunch, though he was schooled from boyhood in the East because his mother, on her deathbed, had wished it. She had never liked the prairies. The wind made her nervous and there were no trees.

John discovers that his return to the West, if only for a vacation, exhilarates him. He tells Serena that he stepped off the train and "everything kind of swung into its place: same stars, same dry, sagey smell, same wide feeling, the way I knew it would be. I felt high as a fool." And he soon finds himself indulging in one of the oldest and most persistent of western fantasies: the idea that the West has the power to make unhappy people happy. "Things were going to be different," he thinks. "Even he and Serena. . . ."

The others, however, are deeply wary of their surroundings. The prairie towns, so provisional-looking and unshaded, carry a "a certain terrible sharpness." And when they leave the prairie behind and ride their horses along piney, light-dappled mountain trails, the beauty is so relentless it becomes monotonous, Walt complains. Above timberline, the peaks surrounding them become a psychic equivalent of the nearby plains: "bare and austere . . . stark and barren." The visitors feel nervous and taxed, even before they see the first wisp of smoke from the forest fire.

There is a tendency among some westerners, perhaps more fierce when this book was written more than half a century ago, to view easterners with a peculiar mixture of envy and disdain. Citizens of the East might know about money and books and power and culture, but they have somehow become atrophied as individuals—so dependent on each other, on talk, and on a mediated experience of the world, that they can't live authentic and capable lives. That attitude (which I state in oversimple terms) clearly interested Walker and may be why she created a counterpoint to the dudes.

He is Burns, their sage and competent guide, and he is big, lean, hard, quiet, deliberate, and adept. Burns looks weathered, but also younger than his years. He is an idealistic loner who never married, he says, because he "wouldn't want any woman unless she wouldn't care whether we lived next to mountains or railroad tracks or whether there was another person in the world as long as there was us. That's love and you don't find it very often."

John remembers that his father once compared Burns to a mountain goat because "not many animals can stand it way up there alone, but . . . goats get down to bare rock and manage to live."

The easterners, on the other hand, are chatty, patronizing, in search of entertainment rather than experience. They are ravenous for the picturesque—"Don't you love the girl over there in jeans with the baby on her shoulder?"—and are constantly trying to capture their surroundings with their movie cameras. It's as if they can't appreciate a place without shaping and containing it—a practice that irritates John and widens the rift between him and Serena.

Introduction

When fire breaks out in the forest, it is likened to the spread of Nazism in Europe, something that seemed controllable for a time but soon grew rampant. In the Montana forest, a change in the direction of the wind fans the blaze into a wall of flame that bears down on John, Walt, Burns, and a forest ranger named Harley—all of them trying to reach a young man they know to be trapped in the drainage where he was cutting logs.

Victor, the European, decides the rescue effort is futile and foolhardy and he returns to camp where the women are. That's when the wind begins to turn for Serena, who finds herself disdaining Victor's tendency to deal with trouble by getting out of its path.

A romantic writer would have used the crisis of the fire and the near-deaths of several of her characters as a chance to deliver resounding epiphanies, crashing insights. (A romantic would also shrivel at Walker's refusal to detach the emotions of sex from the practicalities of it. Serena may be the first out-West character to carry a diaphragm in her backpack.) Walker, however, never reaches for an either/or universe. We are not delivered of a conclusion in which John and Serena are bonded or estranged for all time. We are not encouraged to decide that easterners are bad and westerners are good, or vice versa. She doesn't even allow us to villify Victor, the relativist. She seems, instead, to be asking the reader to be curious and to watch—as she watches—the ways in which the shapes will shift.

Unless the Wind Turns was published in 1941. In her next book, *Winter Wheat*, published in 1944, Walker would move her characters away from the mountains, out onto the Montana plains. In that novel, she is in full sail—writing with confidence and insight about a region and about people that have, by then, become familiar to her. She addresses some of the same themes she raised in *Unless the Wind Turns*: the silences that can rock a marriage; what the American East offers versus what the American West does; and, perhaps most eloquently, how solitary a person can feel on the plains. Sometimes it is an exquisite solitude; sometimes it is the feel of bright freedom; sometimes it is a piercing, wind-in-your-ears aloneness. Walker captured it all.

By rights, Walker's four Montana books should have established her as a major voice of the region. (At this writing, Walker is ninety and lives in Portland, Oregon.) How strange, then, that the massive *A Literary History of the American West*, the standard reference to the region's writers, doesn't so much as mention her in its thirteen hundred–plus pages. Dale Evans and Elizabeth (Mrs. George Armstrong) Custer get index listings, but not Mildred Walker—who wrote nine novels during her twenty-two years in Montana and who was nominated for the National Book Award in 1960.

Perhaps the clue lies in something that happened two years after *Winter Wheat* was published. A. B. Guthrie's *The Big Sky*, published in 1947, gave American readers another, earlier version of Montana: the Montana of the 1830s. Guthrie wrote it, he said, without any intention of romanticizing his characters, especially the mutely tragic mountain man, Boone Caudill. But the fact that he set his drama a century earlier, and that one of its driving themes is the contamination of the wilderness by the hand of man, makes it, *ipso facto*, a romance of a sort. *The Way West*, a sequel to *The Big Sky*, won Guthrie the Pulitzer Prize in 1950. In the 1940s and far beyond—arguably to this day—the version of Montana that entranced most readers was not Mildred Walker's vision of modern Americans working out their relationships with others and with a place. It was Guthrie's vision of an Edenic Montana, always long-gone.

In the 1940s, Mildred Walker knew Guthrie, who had

moved back to the state after many years in the East. She and her husband were friends, too, with Joseph Kinsey Howard, author of another well-known Montana book of the times, *Montana: High, Wide, and Handsome.* They lived very near each other but they weren't, says Walker's daughter, Ripley Hugo, any kind of literary coterie. "They weren't people who talked over their work," she said.

In the 1940s, the decade after *Unless the Wind Turns* was published, Mildred Walker wrote and sold a novel every couple of years. She and her family, during those years, also made regular trips to a little cabin on the south fork of the Teton River that is still used by her children today and that bears more than a passing resemblance to John Davis's hideaway in *Unless the Wind Turns.* The cabin and the Schemms' home in Great Falls are the backdrops in a number of home movies shot by Walker's sister during her visits from the East. Though Walker suggested in *Unless the Wind Turns* that her eastern characters were somewhat ridiculous in the way they interposed movie cameras between themselves and their surroundings, she herself seemed to enjoy the camera's eye.

In those films, we see a handsome, steady-eyed woman with a distinctive, sensual mouth. She is fortyish and walks with a limber, athletic stride. Something, a kind of lanky exuberance, evokes film images of Amelia Earhart. She shepherds her children around her. She triumphantly hoists a dead fish. She waves to the world from atop her cantering horse. Then she disappears—and we get a slow pan of stern grey mountaintops, an endless sweep of grass, no humans, a sunset like streaked blood.

MONDAY

1

"YOU can positively feel the bareness, can't you, Walt?" Lizzie Phillips turned away from the window of the club car with distaste.

"It was just as bare yesterday in North Dakota," her husband objected.

"Yes, but it was new then. It's only the second day that it really sinks in."

"There is certainly plenty of room, but I suppose it isn't easy to support life here," Victor Roth said thoughtfully.

"John doesn't think it's bare," Serena said, looking across at her husband. "I thought he was going to get out and kiss the dirt when we crossed the Dakota-Montana line."

John Davis gave no sign that he had heard.

"Come on, darling, tell them how there's something about it that just gets you." Serena's voice was only half teasing.

3

Sometimes John vowed that he would never tell Serena another opinion or hidden thought. He always heard her telling it later, making a good story of it, and if he called her for it, she was unconscious that it might have hurt.

"I suppose you have to be born out here to like it as well as I do," he said, smiling. You could hardly expect a fancy baby specialist like Walt to take to a man's country. The babies are all born with teeth and spurs out here; no need for pediatricians." He grinned, but he foresaw that he was going to have to defend the country all the time.

"I suppose I must have known it Freshman year, but I'd forgotten that you came from Montana," Walt said, laughing.

"You're not my idea of a rugged Westerner, John!" Lizzie tilted her head on one side as though seeing him in a new light.

"He isn't really. He was born here, but he always went East to school. And after college, we were married and he started making Aero Engines. The only part of Montana I've ever heard him talk about is the mountains. Whenever he was out here, that's where he was," Serena explained.

John signaled the club-car porter abruptly for another drink. He disliked Serena's way of interpreting him. He always had an uncomfortable feeling

that just so she might explain how he felt about
. . . oh, about love or . . . his mind fumbled for
the objects of his deep convictions. He didn't pour
out his ideas to Serena any more. He wondered if
Roth did. Victor was quiet; yet he seemed actively
interested in all that they said. John kept forgetting
that he was a refugee who had left his surgical work
in Vienna after the *Anschluss*.

Walt sprawled comfortably in the chair across the
aisle. "What does Serena mean, you were always in
the mountains, John? You came from Piegan City,
didn't you?"

"Tell them about Burns, John; that's a lovely
story!" Serena interrupted.

John crunched the ice in his mouth. He was getting so that he hated animation in a woman. Lizzie
was animated, too. Neither of them could tell a
thing without setting it off in italics.

"Burns is the wrangler who's going to take us into
the mountains. From what John says, he must be
rare!" Serena raced on.

"Well, just that when I was about seven"—he felt
like a children's storyteller—"my father happened to
be at the station one day back in 1919. . . ."

"Seven in 1919 makes you twenty-nine, my boy,"
Walt interpolated.

John made a face at him. "As I was saying, he

was at the station when Burns stepped off the train. Burns had been in the 119th Infantry and was almost the first soldier home. Dad went up and welcomed him, and it seems that Burns had gotten off the boat and taken the first train for Montana; hadn't stopped for a thing. Dad asked him if he didn't want to look New York over or see a few things first, and he said that the part of the world that meant most to him right then was his own shack in the mountains in Elkhorn County, Montana."

"Now that's what I call the adventurous spirit!" Lizzie said derisively.

"Oh, I can understand that," Victor murmured.

"I'll be darned! Seen enough, I suppose," Walt commented. "The 119th saw plenty; lots of them never got back."

"Well, anyway," John went on, "that pleased Dad. He thought his town and his state were just about right, and loyalty to them would excuse a man in his eyes for any minor sins like thieving or adultery. So that summer, of course, he took me out to Burns and told him to take me over and teach me to ride and fish and know the mountains. Burns was making his living by trapping and taking parties out in the mountains."

"Oh, but that isn't the cute part, John! His father

went panting right back from the station to the Rotary luncheon and made a speech about Burns." Serena enlarged on it: "If you could have seen a picture of John's father; he was a great big, gruff old codger with a profile as rugged as a mountain cliff!" Serena's tone was possessive and at the same time patronizing, John thought with irritation.

"Your old man probably thought you'd love the town and the state, too," Walt said.

John's mouth twisted. "I suppose." As far as he could see out the window no mountains were visible, but they were over there. That was what made the country different from the Dakotas. Well, they did mean something to him, something that had brought him back this year.

"I'm certainly anxious to see this Burns man," Lizzie said.

"Sounds like quite a guy," Walt added. "George Gray asked me the other day why on earth we were going to Montana, and I said it was a long story but it had to do with a glass of sherry before dinner back in February, and he said it sounded to him like the start of a first-class mystery."

"Wasn't it funny the way we went over to your house that night, Serena, without an idea but that we'd go to the Cape as usual and came away with a trip to Montana planned?" Lizzie went on.

7

"That's the way to do things. I adore plans on the spur of the moment," Serena gloated.

"It is more amusing, still, that you should have invited me to join you," Victor said. His English was perfect, his slight accent not unpleasant.

John Davis lighted a cigarette calmly enough, but he squirmed the toe of his shoe irritably against the heavy Pullman carpet of the club car. Damn the blindheadedness of people anyway! All three of them, Lizzie and Walt and Victor, figured he was pleased pink to have them along. Serena was; that was the trouble. He had planned the trip just for the two of them. For the first summer since they'd been married he was going where he wanted to go with Serena, alone. And then, by God, it had turned out that they weren't going alone.

It had developed as neatly as though they were acting a play; they were having sherry before dinner. Walt had asked of no one in particular, "What are you going to do this summer?" But Serena answered; Serena usually did.

"Oh, John's dragging me off out West. We're going to do a sentimental pilgrimage to the scenes of his childhood."

"Going to point out every stick and stone to her," he had played up. "After all, she married a man from Montana."

Everyone had laughed. "John, you're a scream. Can you sing *Home on the Range?*" Lizzie had asked.

And then he had heard Serena saying, "Listen, why don't you all come along? John and I are going to take horses and pack in. We could get someone to go along and do the cooking. We'd have a wonderful time! And it would be such a new experience for Vic. Do you go on pack trips in Austria, Vic?"

"Not on horses. I've climbed in the Alps a good deal."

It had rolled up like that. Serena had no idea that something had been spoiled; that he had wanted to go away just with her; that that was the whole point of the trip.

"We get off this train in fifteen minutes and take a funny little train to Sweet Springs," Serena told them. "Let's go back, Lizzie, and put on our hats." Serena had the details of the trip as well in mind as though she had made it before. "I want to see if that porter feels better. He looked so sick this morning when he was making up the berths that I asked him how he felt. He said he'd just gotten over the flu."

"And I came in and found S'rena helping him with the berths!" John said. That was Serena for you, always thoughtful of servants and employees, and curiously thoughtless where he was concerned.

"Anyone could see he was sick," Serena insisted.

John watched her, walking through the car. He felt a shade of relief that she had left. She was so sure of herself, so . . . complacent. He studied the carriage of her head and shoulders; her slim, tall body. Lizzie steadied herself; Serena walked confidently, in spite of the swaying train.

Sometimes he wondered if anything in her life had ever made her wonder if she were wrong; if, for example, she had married the wrong man. But, of course, she would never admit that. And, if she found some lack in him, there was Victor.

"We've got time for one more," Walt said. "I'm just beginning to relax and realize that I'm on a vacation. All the way out here I've been holding myself tense, expecting a call from the hospital about some sick child."

John grinned. "It doesn't hurt my feelings to think that we're going out where you couldn't sell an airplane motor if you tried."

For an unexpected minute they were still, each busy with his own thinking.

"A vacation's a funny thing, you know it?" Walt said.

"My Dad used to pride himself on the fact that he never took any. Hell, his whole life was a vacation in a way; he got such a kick out of the mill and town. I only heard him say once that he wished he hadn't stuck so close to the mill," John said.

"Mhmm. A vacation and a honeymoon; a man's never quite natural on either one," Walt added. "The best vacation's the kind that gives you an illusion of being busier than all get out."

Victor laughed. "Now you're living up to the European concept of the American business-man, as substantiated in Mr. Lewis' writings. You don't often, you know."

"How do you mean, Victor? Oh, about vacations," Walt said.

"We won't be so busy on this one, but we'll keep moving," John said. He felt suddenly eager to be there.

2

THE stub-line train pulled into Sweet Springs, Montana, a little before noon; not swiftly, conclusively, but shuffling softly until it came to a stop, as though its inner impetus had given out. The rails that had marched parallel across the spaces of the prairie were suddenly broken off a little beyond the station platform, the ends rusting in clumps of sagebrush.

A small flurry of activity blew up around the ugly, orange-painted station. One limp bag of mail was thrown off on the platform, one additional passenger dismounted, and the five in city clothes who were obviously dudes.

The station agent looked at them with mild curiosity. The driver of the bus loitered a few minutes while he rolled himself a cigarette and then, deciding they were not fares, drove off noisily. The movement of the bus stirred the yellow leaves of the cottonwoods that had fallen on the ground. Grasshoppers jumped across the cinder track and lighted on the dusty grass of the station yard and the flurry of activity subsided for another day.

"You waiting for someone?" the station agent asked.

"Yes." John walked over to him. "You're Mr. Howe, aren't you? I used to come up here summers when I was a boy. I'm John Davis."

"Jack's boy! 'Course. You look a little like the old man, at that," he said, shaking his hand. "Going back in the mountains?"

"Yes, with Burns."

"It's a little early for hunting."

"We're just going in for a pack trip. It seems good to be back here."

"The home-coming!" Walt murmured to the others.

"Would you call the station Gothic?" Lizzie asked, squinting at the orange frame building.

"How about that grain elevator!" Serena said, nodding across the tracks where a single angular building cut its height into the sky. Across the gray boards faded letters read "J. A. Davis Milling Co."

"John's father!" Walt cried delightedly.

"Of course," Serena said. "John used to talk about

coming back here and going in business with his father after college."

"That would have been somep'n! I can see you here, Serena," Lizzie jeered.

The rattletrap car that came for them was driven by a lanky boy in jeans. In his wide-brimmed hat and high-heeled boots, the boy might have been himself ten years ago, John thought. He used to drive to town for Burns.

"I'm sorry you had to wait. Burns' watch stopped," the boy explained.

John grinned. "When did Burns start carrying a watch?"

Walt laughed. Unconsciously, he glanced at the watch on his wrist. It was twelve minutes to twelve.

"Burns said for you to drive 'em out. I'm going to catch a ride out tomorrow. He said you'd ought to remember the holes in the road. I'll ride as far as Main Street with you."

Main Street lay hot and quiet under the September sun. The old cottonwood trees threw a lazy shade across the dirt street. Wooden buildings with high false fronts lined the business block.

"It's been plenty dry," the boy said. "Some bad fires over in the Tenderfoot. Burns said to tell you he'd have dinner waiting for you. Well, so long." He swung off the running board, touching his hat.

Monday

"Look! Don't you love the girl over there in jeans with the baby on her shoulder?" Lizzie said.

"I can count six beer places on one street. On a Saturday night this street might be fairly lively," Walt commented.

"Don't worry, this is an old cattle town that's seen plenty of excitement and still does at times," John said.

"Lynn Fontanne and Alfred Lunt in *Reunion in Vienna*," Serena read from the sign over the one movie house. "That's for you, Victor! Can you think of anything farther from the comprehension of people living in a place like this!"

Victor smiled. "That was a good film. I saw it."

"There you are, Walt!" Lizzie pointed out the doctor's sign on a gate. "How would you like to be practicing here?"

"No, thank you!"

"We'll change our clothes and leave our city stuff here in the hotel," John said. He parked the car before the shabby front of the Montana House. "Make it snappy. We've got twenty miles to drive before we eat."

They stopped for a coke in the drugstore before they left, standing at the fountain in their new jeans and bandannas that smelled of a dry-goods store. Serena and Lizzie had spent a summer at a dude ranch in Wyoming, and Walt had been to Sun Valley, but the clothes they had, their belts and Stetsons and Serena's beaded jacket, were fancy for Sweet Springs. People stared at them as they walked along the street. A boy on the corner called out, "Where's the Rodeo at?"

"John, you're having a chocolate soda! How precious!" Lizzie exclaimed gleefully.

"Want a sip?" John sucked the sickly sweet, cold liquid and wondered if it tasted the same as it did fifteen years ago.

From where he stood he could see the grain elevator across the tracks. He used to think grain elevators were ugly eyesores, but today the big wooden bulk with J. A. Davis still showing on it seemed to mean something to him. He remembered his father saying, "They're the Hudson Bay Posts of my generation, John."

Then he remembered that the J. A. Davis didn't mean anything any more. His father had sold out to an Eastern elevator company. The larger concern had only left the name there to fade off.

And here was J. A. Davis' son, back with a bunch of dudes who were going into the mountains because it was something to do.

He set his soda glass down on the pink imitation-marble counter.

Monday

"Ready?" He noticed as he went out that you could still buy the Sunday edition of the *Denver Post,* with its vivid feature section and pages of comics. He used to lie on his bunk and read every word.

They rattled out of town, past the museum and the general store and the movie and the beer halls, beyond the stark shadow of the grain elevator, toward the mountains.

"The houses look as flimsy as the cardboard ones we used to get to cut out, don't they?" Lizzie said. "I'm warning you, Walt, if you ever went to practicing in a town like this I'd do a Madame Bovary!"

"And this is all part of the great American scene!" Victor said, smiling at her.

"You're damn right it is!" John heard himself saying overemphatically. He had no brief for it. It was just coming back after so long that made him feel so foolishly loyal. "Of course, I never stayed in it much longer than this at any one time," he confessed with a laugh. "Look there." Ahead of them, without introduction or warning, reared a long line of mountains.

"Them there's mountains!" Walt said.

"We head straight for that notch," John told them happily.

They fell silent watching the jagged line of blue

piled peaks, streaked at the top with snow. John drove with his old Stetson pulled down against the sun, his eyes narrow and gray on the view ahead. Just seeing the mountains again, standing there without changing: the Twin Maidens and the Saw Tooth and old Hungry Man Mountain, same as ever, rested him. There weren't so many things you could be sure of. Politics, love . . . had a way of being a lot of different things under a lot of different names, but the mountains he was sure of. He let the sun-baked ruts take the wheels and joggle the car.

"John! For Heaven's sake, what if I had false teeth?" Lizzie shrieked from the back seat.

"Bite down hard, baby!" John called back. He felt suddenly hilarious.

Walt was in the front seat with him. Victor sat between the girls in back. Walt moved his arm along the back of the seat so his hand lay on John's shoulder.

"Kinda like being back here?" Walt asked, digging his shoulder affectionately.

Serena sat forward watching the road that was only a faint track across the flats. She hadn't been so keen about this trip at first, but now that they were really started she was anxious to arrive, to see Burns, to start out. She ought to get some wonderful movies. She glanced back to make sure her camera paraphernalia was all there and then looked over at Victor. He was looking at his light meter. He shook his head.

"Too far away; wouldn't show much."

She was glad he had come.

Lizzie made a sudden dive down at her feet. "Where is . . . oh! Here it is." She came up with her portable radio. She snapped on the dial. There was a crackling sound, louder than the rattle of the car.

"Be in the know with Texaco!"

"Lizzie, for Pete's sake!" Serena complained.

"Turn off that thing!" John bellowed.

"Be still, children; it's the news," Lizzie said. "I thought you'd want to hear it."

"I can do without it for a little, thanks," John muttered.

"Shall I throw it out, John? Leave it to rust on the plains along with the oxcarts and the bones the other pioneers left behind them?" Walt asked.

"As long as it's there we could hear it," Victor said soothingly.

John accelerated, driving over the flats so fast the loose stones flew up against the fenders. Grasshoppers smeared themselves against the windshield. The car rattled in every part. But above the clatter came the insistent voice reporting the news, and out of habit they strained to hear.

Lizzie turned the radio off. Of a sudden the world seemed emptied of sound. As though, momentarily deafened, they could only stare like children out the car windows. The twists in the road had slowed the car. Clumps of sagebrush and gnarled jack pine threw deep shadows under the strong noon sun. The brightness of the sky bore down on them, as though they had not seen it while they were listening to the radio. The phrases from the news shimmered in the hot air. Then, slowly, the creek sounds, imperceptible at first, swelled to a roar. A chicken hawk's wing beat loudly against the air. A gopher pierced their eardrums with his shrill cry.

"It is not good to hear the news; it makes you feel guilty coming off on a pleasure trip to the mountains," Victor said quietly.

"Why not; you can't do anything about it right now. If we were there, it would be different. Sometimes I envy women in England. They have something to do; something that matters, I mean," Serena said impulsively.

Then the car left the flats and turned into the narrow canyon road. Coolness, like an answer, rushed down to them from the high rocky banks; from the shadows under the fir trees, and the soft color of the cedars and the green-brown floor of the stream. Twice they had to ford the stream, then the road climbed up from the creek as though it were clinging to the steep wall of the reef.

"A handful of men could defend this against a whole army; you know that?" Walt said.

John nodded. The road was no better than it used to be, he noted with satisfaction.

"Hold her, Newt!" Walt groaned as he looked down into the stream bed.

John was watching for the first sign of Burns' cabin. He hardly heard the others. Behind those aspens. . . . He glanced quickly to see that they still shimmered. He shifted into first again. The car bumped over the ridge of rock that no gravel or mud or sand ever covered, and came to a stop in front of the log cabin and corral.

"Here we are," John said, staring at the sagging plank steps of the porch and the antlers piled at one side. He was back. He couldn't feel it yet. He must talk now, make sure they liked it. Where was Burns?

A girl came out of the cabin, banging the screen door behind her; a girl in faded jeans and a shirt that hung out over her pants. Soft light hair framed her face, but was caught up in back in tin curlers.

"H'lo," she said, nodding at them. She walked to

the end of the porch and called back toward the root cellar that ran into the side hill.

"Burns, the dudes are here."

It was queer to see a woman around Burns' place. "She must cook for him," John said to the others, but he was annoyed that anything should be altered and relieved when the girl, without another word, disappeared inside. Then he saw Burns. He needn't have worried. Burns was the same as ever, even to the old hat that shaded his face. He looked too big for the small log cabin, just as he always did.

"Hi, Burns!" John called out.

"Hi, boy." Burns' voice slipped again into John's mind as naturally as a leather strap into its buckle. John introduced the others, but he was thinking of Burns' voice coming out of an early morning mist on a hunting trip, out of the dark, riding down the side of the mountain, soft and slow like that even when he was cussing him out for letting a horse break his bridle. The voices of the others sounded thin and loud beside it.

"I'm sure pleased to meet you folks," Burns was saying. "Come right in and I'll get you some dinner before we start out."

The log cabin was smaller and darker than ever. It had seemed big and gloomy that first time when he was nine. The great bearskin stretched on the end wall had bristled then. Now he noticed how one edge curled over showing the papery underskin. He wondered how Burns kept the moths out of it. Serena made such a fuss over the white fur rug at home.

"Sit down, sit down," Burns urged. He, himself, threw one leg over a long bench, sitting on it as though it were a saddle. His fingers reached for the bag of Bull Durham in the pocket of his flannel shirt. Burns was as lean and hard as ever; his movements were as slow and quiet as John had remembered. He never seemed in a hurry. Through the open door they could see the girl moving around in the kitchen lean-to, setting the table.

"Well, sir, back in the winter when I got John's letter I thought you'd change your mind by summer," Burns said. "Had a party of men coming out from Boston for sure, but with the war they got scared. Thought they'd better stay home and watch their traps. Matter of fact, if the world's going to fall to pieces they might better be off up here with a good horse under 'em."

"John," Serena came over to him on the pretext of wanting a match. She spoke in a low voice. "John, what about dinner? After all, we ordered in advance and he said he'd have it waiting for us."

John grinned. "Unlax! You're not at the country

club, and Burns is no dining-room steward. This is just his way; he never hurries," he murmured, holding a light for Serena's cigarette.

"Well, folks, if you're going to eat I better move around and help my second cook. Rose, come in here and meet these people."

The girl came, looking at them without any sign of interest or curiosity.

"This is Rose Logan," Burns said. "Her man, Mike, is up in the woods cutting logs to make 'em a cabin."

"Pleased to meet you," Rose answered, unsmiling.

"Rose is about to pine away, staying down here with me," Burns chuckled. "She ain't been married a year yet. That right, Rose?"

The girl nodded.

"Well, c'mon, Rose, we'll go get dinner."

Serena watched Burns lift the lid of the stove and apply a match. "John, he hasn't even got the fire going." Serena's irritation showed in the way she put out her half-smoked cigarette. She felt as responsible as though she were the hostess.

John, himself, slipped with a kind of unholy glee back into this world where there was no time; where everything was easygoing and inefficient except where it mattered, like throwing a proper diamond hitch to hold a pack safely or cooking a meal in the rain. He laughed an irritating, delighted laugh.

"Let's play some bridge," Lizzie suggested. "Come on, Walt."

"Vic, wanta play?" Serena asked. Victor was looking in the glass cabinet Burns had filled with trophies. John had looked at them so many times on rainy days he could have named off every one from the cast-off rattles to the gold dust Burns had panned out of the Turtle River. He felt a foolish flash of annoyance that Victor should be looking them over.

"You four play," Victor urged politely.

"I'm going out to talk to Burns," John said. He didn't want to play bridge the first half hour that they were back here in the mountains.

"Come on, Vic; John never wants to," Serena said.

John's annoyance at Serena rose. He ambled carelessly out to sit on the woodbox by the cookstove, where he could watch Burns' deliberate movements. The girl leaned on the window sill, not seeming to look at either of them.

"Well, boy, you're back!" Burns said over the sound of the frying. His long face wrinkled into a warm grin.

"Yep," John answered. "It's been a long time."

"Six years," Burns said promptly. "You were back last the time your old man died."

"That was in March," John remembered.

"Best month of the whole year in the mountains," Burns said, sticking the pot-holder in his hip pocket, rolling himself another cigarette. "Still as summer up here, an' if it does get cold there's the chinooks."

John shook his head. "I like it best this time of year."

"Nope," Burns said decisively. "It's too dry. It's been the dryest summer we've had in years."

"Mike says it's so dry up at Bear Creek there ain't any creek at all, hardly," the girl said suddenly. "It's hot, too. He sweats so it seems his shirts would rot away. I wish I'd gone with him, though."

It was as though, once started talking, words kept coming from her. Then she picked up a pail and dipper, and went out toward the spring. John resented her being there and was glad when she had gone.

"She's the lonesomest kid you ever saw," Burns explained. "I kinda hate to leave her here alone while we go off, but her husband'll be back down here in a couple a weeks. They're both nothing but kids; crazy about each other!" Burns waved his pancake turner to emphasize his remark.

"Wonderful, Vic! I thought you'd go down one." Serena's voice came out to the kitchen, followed by Walt's laugh. They might as well have been at home. They would carry their own color into the mountains, making this trip something else: Lizzie with her radio, and Serena with her cards and Victor to talk to and romanticize about. John wished to heaven he'd come off up here alone.

Burns was sliding the fish onto a platter. Rose brought a bowl of water cress and set down the bottle of Heinz vinegar and a can of vegetable oil beside it. That would get Serena, John thought. Serena always had to have pure olive oil. She'd eat hers with salt and pepper, even as she was praising the meal.

"That looks good, Burns," John said. "Nobody fries potatoes and trout the way you do."

"I guess we're ready." Burns cast a glance at the oilcloth table. "Rose, we better have some butter on here."

They filled the table in Burns' kitchen; the five of them and Burns and Rose. John wondered with secret amusement what Serena thought about Rose, about her tin curlers and the shirt that hung out over her jeans. Serena ignored her, leaning past her to talk to Burns.

"Do you really think we'll see some mountain goats, Burns? John used to boast about being so high in the mountains he could hear the goats rolling rocks down. Well, that's what he said!" she insisted as they all joined in the laugh at his expense, except Rose and Burns.

On a sudden impulse, formed partly from annoyance with the others, partly because they ignored Rose so completely, John turned to her:

"Rose, I can see that your mind is up at Bear Creek with Mike. Why don't you come along with us? We're going right up Bear Creek, and you can stay with your husband while we go on up to the Chinese Wall and then come back down with us."

The girl's face brightened wonderfully. She plucked nervously at the top button of her shirt. "That would be swell. I'd sure like to see Mike." She laughed a foolish, thin little laugh. "I guess he'd like to see me, too."

John avoided looking at the others. He applied himself assiduously to boning his trout. "Fine! Burns, you'll fix Rose up with a horse, won't you?"

"She's got her own, one she broke herself. She's had a notion before this to ride up there on her own, but I've kept her here. I've got enough blankets and provisions in. All you'll have to take, Rose, 'll be your toothbrush."

"Good. Let's see, Rose, you don't know the names of these people you're going with." John made his voice heartier than was natural, taking a malicious pleasure in the sharp silence around the table. "This is Elizabeth Phillips, known as Lizzie, and her husband, Dr. Walt Phillips. This is Dr. Victor Roth, known as Vic . . ." that was something, since he himself still avoided calling Roth by his first name, "and my wife, Serena." There, let them have it; the spirit of the West and all that sort of thing!

Rose looked at each one in turn, smiling only faintly.

"You've got enough doctors in your party, anyway," she said.

They laughed politely. Once John met Serena's eye. She looked back steadily, holding his eyes overlong. She was very angry. Why should she be? She had invited Lizzie and Walt and Victor Roth without asking his permission. He could invite someone, too. The trip was something else from what he had planned; it didn't matter who was along now. He would devote himself to Rose. She didn't need to bother them.

He wondered what Burns was thinking. He thought he detected a twinkle in Burns' eyes, but he couldn't be sure, any more than you could tell whether a horse was grinning when he bucked you off.

"Well, I'll go pack your duffle." Burns drank down the rest of his coffee and stood up. "Rose, you can put away the food here, and wash up the dishes."

The rest followed out to the corral. John saw Burns waiting for Lizzie's and Walt's stuff, looking with mild amusement at the jars of sunburn cream, the bottle of mineral oil, the stuff for Walt's hair, six changes of underwear, and the radio.

"You won't need half of that stuff, Ma'm; it'll just be a bother to you when we go to make camp some night in the dark. But we'll pack 'em for you if you think you want 'em."

And then John lost himself in the business of helping Burns saddle and pack the horses.

"You're to ride Flash, boy," Burns said quietly, and the years rolled back. There was always a Flash in Burns' string of horses. "I broke her this spring, and she's plenty frisky."

John found himself as secretly elated as when he was eleven and Burns had let him ride another three-year-old Flash.

The ground of the corral, made of horse manure and sawdust and mountain soil, was soft under his feet. The sun beat down on his shoulders, and on his hands that were so white and soft as they pulled the cinch tight.

"Whoa, girl." He made little sounds in his throat, copying Burns. "You see, you slip this over the head . . ." he was showing Victor and Walt as Burns had taught him years ago. Walt might be the smartest young pediatrician at Children's Hospital, but here he was all thumbs; and Victor wasn't so hot either! He wondered if Serena saw him throw the diamond on Alabama, the old pack horse.

"You haven't forgot, have you, boy," Burns said quietly behind him.

"When do we start?" Lizzie was asking, her vivacious face pouted with pretty impatience.

Where was Serena, John wondered. Then he saw her sitting over on the steps taking moving pictures of them all. Seeing her there threw the whole trip back into perspective. It was no longer life itself; it was just a stunt they did one summer. He could feel himself back in Serena's pink and white and green living room, replete with dinner, drinking coffee and a liqueur, Serena saying, "You haven't seen the pictures of our trip in the Rockies last summer, have you?" People's polite murmur of simulated interest.

He went inside the log stable after a saddle for Bareface. Serena would say, "There's John disappearing in the stable. Honestly, you'd have thought he was a cowboy, himself!" The laughter. Serena always kept up a line of chatter when she showed her pictures.

"You wouldn't think it would be this hot in September, would you?" Lizzie exclaimed, wiping her face with her brand-new red bandanna.

"It shouldn't be. It's immoral," Walt said.

John could see how angry Serena was with him over his asking Rose by the heightened color in her cheeks. He waited for her to come over to him. Instead she stayed away, ignoring him. That was her way, too, when she was angry.

Rose finished her work in the cabin and came across to the corral. She carried only a small bundle rolled in a slicker. She had taken the curlers out and tied a bandanna over her head. But the blue shirt still hung out over her jeans. As though she sensed that she was not entirely welcome, she went directly to her horse and tied the bundle back of the saddle.

"That's a nice pony you have," John said to her because no one else said anything.

Again her face broke into a smile. "Mike gave him to me. He's got the father; his name's Pay Dirt."

"All right, I guess we're off. You lead the way, John, and I'll bring up the rear," Burns directed.

They started around past the corral, up the trail that climbed along the canyon wall back of the cabin. John, then Serena, then Victor, then Lizzie and Walt and Rose. Now that they were on their way, John forgot his irritation. He had almost forgotten how he loved this place. How blue the sky could be and the air so clear your eye could pick out the first turning of an aspen tree over on the other side of the canyon. For three weeks nothing would bother him. He reached over to straighten Flash's forelock under her bridle.

"Hi-yi-ee!" he called back to Burns, his voice filling the canyon. A marmot scuttled into his hole at the sound, and a camp robber flashed in gray anger across the trail, shrilling out his hoarse cry of warning as he flew.

3

"YOUR wives are a couple of nesters, not open-range grazers at all," Burns said to John and Walt as the men stood around the fire. Back of them on the hill they could just make out Lizzie and Serena's location by the sudden gleams of their flashlights. The girls had deserted the fire and taken their sleeping bags up on the hill. Rose had made a bed for herself at a little distance from the fire.

"Your wife was smart, John; she lugged her stuff up on that knoll where she'll get the eastern sun."

"Lizzie's got us so close to the creek I'm afraid we'll roll in if we're restless in our sleep," Walt laughed. "Gosh, I'm lame. How far did we make, Burns?"

"Just ten miles, but we started late. I figgered we better start easy."

"Easy! Oh, my soul, John! Tell him we weren't born in Montana."

34

"I find myself more than a little lame, too," Victor said. "But it is pleasant. Since coming to America I have had little exercise."

Burns pushed a long log farther into the fire and brought a pine knot to drop on the fresh flames. Then he sat down again and rolled himself another cigarette. His quick eyes were on Victor.

"Serena tells me you only just got out of Austro-Hungary in time; climbed out halfway across the Alps."

Serena had made sure Burns saw Victor in a colorful light, John thought. He wondered when she had found the chance.

"Yes, some friends warned me in time. When the *Anschluss* people found how I felt about them, they started to hunt me down as though I were a Jew."

Burns shook his head. "We should have done a better job of it when we were there in 1918. How did you get over here?"

"I managed to get to Paris. I had friends there who helped me to secure a passport. Now my friends there need help."

John noticed how Victor answered all questions put to him with unfailing courtesy, but with a kind of finality that discouraged further questions. He liked Victor, what he had seen of him. He would have liked him better if Serena had not taken him up so hard. He wondered what Victor thought of Serena. He was doubtless grateful to her. Serena had helped him find an apartment and had secured several engagements for him to speak where he could raise money to send back home. Walt and Lizzie and Serena had opened all kinds of doors to him. And he had, in return, made Serena's winter for her.

John studied him, sitting across the fire from Burns. They were a complete contrast. Burns was big and raw-boned, with an unruly head of blonde hair. He was over six feet tall, with large hands and feet and a thin neck, reddened by the weather. His eyes were blue and sharp, and he had a laugh with body to it. He was over fifty, but he looked no more than forty. Victor was dark. The firelight gave his skin more color than it possessed of itself. He was nearly as tall as Burns, but the smaller features of his face, his small hands and feet, made him seem shorter. He was thirty, Serena said, but he looked older. Walt looked like an interne beside him. All the animation of his face centered in his dark eyes. He spoke in a slightly precise tone that gave his words unusual articulation.

Serena had said, "Think what good it will do him to go on a trip like that!"

Walt had been pleased to have him, too. Walt said he was plenty keen in his work; had some articles in

American as well as foreign journals and was a real addition to the department at Bellevue, where he had a small place at a small salary.

John had seen him several times, at the house for dinner and over at Walt's, but he still reserved his judgment. After this trip he would know how he liked him; if he could separate him from Serena, that is.

"Well," Walt said, "I guess I'll take my weary bones to bed if we're going to do more riding tomorrow." But he didn't move.

The bell on the lead horse came down to them close by. John remembered how the horses were always away the minute you took their saddles off and then drifted back near to camp by themselves, as though they hankered after human companionship, after all.

"Awful close for a night in the mountains," Burns said. "Tomorrow on the trail you don't want to do any smoking, or if you do, you want to know where every spark goes. The forest rangers ain't letting any campers out without a guide with 'em since the woods are so dry."

Walt laughed. "This isn't close to us after New York."

"That closeness in the city is the thing I find it so hard to grow accustomed to," Victor said.

"Around Vienna we have the Wienerwald, tree-covered mountains similar to these, which give a coolness. But here the closeness only draws the sweet night around you more tightly."

John dug the loose dirt from along the edge of his boot with a match stick. That was what Serena liked about Victor; his sudden lapses into speech that were like poetry embarrassed him, yet they were true enough. The closeness did bring the smell of the fire and the sagebrush nearer. The creek noise was loud tonight. If you listened long enough, it sounded like two people talking.

"I'm going this time!" Walt got up and John followed him.

"I'll call you in the morning, boy, in time to get the horses!" Burns told John.

"Say, I'll be up before you are!" John retorted. "Don't roll into the creek!" he called out to Walt and Lizzie. "Got enough blankets?"

"Snug as a bug," Lizzie called back.

"How about you, Rose?" After all, it was his trip and he was responsible for everyone.

Walking up the little hill where Serena had put their bed rolls seemed like going upstairs to their bedroom. Even out here in the mountains the queer stilted way he had come to feel about Serena followed him, giving this hill under the wide night sky the feeling of walls and moods. Tonight, Serena would have plenty to say about his asking Rose. He kicked at the dirt with his toe and stood still, taking a long breath to fill his lungs and mind with the mountain air.

Up here the aspens seemed to make a louder rustling. He was glad they had come out here in September. They would see the aspens turn, unless it was an unusualy late fall. These yellows and apricot shades and the dark red of the brush, Oregon grape and kinni-kinnick and the yellow willows—he named them over to himself, liking the names—these were more to him than the vivid fall colors in New England that Serena loved so. He didn't know why; just stubborn, maybe. In the East, at school, he used to walk through the village and look at all the maples, bright red and yellow on the same tree, and the woodbine, crimson over the woodsheds. Boys, the little fellows, used to collect the bright leaves and press them in books. He used to press a yellow leaf sometimes, never a red one. The yellow ones made him think of the aspens back here: quakers, Burns called them. They stood in tribes, like Indians, yellow to copper-colored, but none deeper. The leaves hadn't turned yet, but already there was a dead-leaf smell, rich and musky in the air. He breathed it in happily. It was the same, after all. Eagerness stirred in him. Things were going to be different out here. Even he and Serena. . . .

He came quietly, his old moccasin boots making no sound. "Hello, squaw-woman." His voice was gentle.

"Hello," Serena answered. "I feel like a squaw-woman. I just dug a rock out from under my sleeping bag. I'm ready to turn in. Want the flash?"

"Nope. I'd rather let my eyes get used to the dark. That first summer out here, when I was nine, I was scared all the time darting around with a flashlight. And then the battery wore out, and I got used to going around in the dark. Things don't pop out at you and look so strange as they do when you have a light to throw on them." He sat down on the edge of his bed roll, annoyed with himself. Now why had he gone on about a flashlight? That wasn't what he wanted to say. He wanted to tell Serena how he felt.

"Listen, S'rena, I started out this morning being angry. The more I thought about your bringing Walt and Lizzie and this refugee of yours along so you wouldn't be alone with me, the madder I got."

"But, John, that's such a childish attitude. . . ."

"Wait, let me finish. All of a sudden, walking up the hill from the fire, I wasn't angry. Everything kind of swung into its place: same stars, same dry, sagey smell, same wide feeling, the way I knew it would be. I felt high as a fool. I could laugh at myself for being so angry about the others. I don't care if they are along; you're here."

Serena started to speak.

"Don't," John said. "I don't want to know that there's anybody here but ourselves for a little; do you see, S'rena? Up here in the mountains things are going to be different for us. S'rena, I want to love you, up here where I used to think what loving a woman would be like. I used to read books and wonder if it was really like that . . . kinda simpleminded, maybe.

"I want to love you without talking too much about it, without being so everlastingly careful. Suppose you did get pregnant! That's part of it. Maybe that's one of the things that's wrong with us, that we don't want to risk anything until it's convenient. Good God, when would it be convenient?

"I've been a droopy fool these last weeks. I've been muzzing around about the emptiness of our life and the futility of making Aero Engines. I've wished to heaven I'd come back out here and taken up Dad's business; at least, it would be helping to feed people. I've even blamed you in my mind for keeping me from it. But that's not the trouble; the whole thing is our getting so far away from each other; thinking we don't matter to each other. I was crazy, S'rena."

He laughed in relief as he said it so the words came out aloud in the night. He leaned above her.

"Love me, S'rena, not the way we usually do." He kissed her hard on the lips and burrowed his head in her shoulder. He didn't want her to speak, to dim the clear sure need he felt. If he could only show her how he felt.

"But, John . . . ," Serena's voice was tolerant, cool. "I've always . . ."

He stopped her words again with his mouth on hers. She mustn't; he'd lose this feeling of sureness, even this wanting. If she discussed it, she could cool the desire in him until loving was just an act, a natural, normal, married act. He couldn't explain to her, he must just carry her with him. He let his hands try to tell her and his body press against hers. He thought he felt her hands tighten on his shoulders, and the desire in him swelled triumphantly.

"S'rena," he whispered as though that was all there was to say. "Oh, S'rena!" He stood up to drop off his clothes, like some coarse wrapping. The hot, dark wind touched his skin. Eagerness ran in him like a stream. He hadn't felt like this since . . . he stopped his mind. He mustn't stop to think. He kicked off his shoes and was aware of the delicate feeling of the dry, grizzled grass under his feet.

"S'rena," he whispered, lying down beside her.

"John, listen to me a minute." Serena spoke in a tone of voice that seemed too loud up on the hill. "I'll let you love me because we haven't for so long, but don't ever be so childish again: going off to the kitchen and talking with Burns as though nobody else was around, and then asking that terrible girl to come with us, just to get back at me. That was pretty poor."

He hardly heard her words at first, only the tone of voice separating them, as it had so often. Cruelly, the eagerness died in him. The perspiration that had sprung freely along his skin dried in the air. He felt the weariness of his body a dead weight on the ground. He was lying so close to Serena the flannel sleeve of her pajama touched him. He moved away.

She was sitting up, rummaging in the pack beside her.

"We don't want to take a chance just now on my being pregnant."

He knew the sound of the box lid. The faint medicinal, almost pleasant odor that cut across the soft sage smell. It wasn't unlike the antiphlogistin smell he remembered in his childhood. He reached for his clothes, feeling himself grotesque sprawling naked on the warm ground.

"John!" Serena's tone was imperious, conscious of

her generosity. His mind recoiled fiercely from her passive willingness of body. There was no eagerness or need of the spirit.

"You know you're awfully unreasonable, John." Her tone was impatient now.

He pulled on his jeans and shirt and woolen socks, not caring that his movements were loud in the stillness.

"Skip it," he said finally, hoping it sounded carelessly flippant.

Slowly his mind that had been merged in the feeling of his body separated itself. He didn't bother to lie on his sleeping bag, liking the hard ground.

"Well, of course, if you're going to be temperamental," Serena said, not finishing her sentence. He listened to the sound of her movements as she prepared for bed again.

He lay still, trying not to stir his mind into activity, but it was no use. He rested his head on his arms and looked at the stars. There was no help in them; they were too far away. They had seen too many human beings to be stirred by the pitiful fiascos humans made of their lives. A phrase came into his head: "Most men lead lives of quiet desperation." He'd read it in a *Reader's Digest,* lying in the twin bed beside Serena. Thoreau had written that.

Monday

"Don't you think you better turn out the light? We were up so late last night, John!" Serena had said just as he finished reading it. He remembered. He had turned out the light and opened the windows. He had stopped to kiss her goodnight and afterward, in the dark, he had lain there, hating his life, his and Serena's together.

He had taken himself in hand, he remembered. There must be millions of men and women like himself; people who have work and food and health, and still feel that way. The words fitted the picture: nothing violent or vulgar or positive, just the dull aching sense of missing out, of not getting anywhere. He and Serena; he couldn't mean very much to her; he must make her mean less to him.

Tonight, they might as well have been at home. They had turned the hill into their bedroom. They lay side by side, worlds apart. At home when they talked, their voices came out hard and separate. Their words cut into the dark like scissors making fancy patterns out of paper. Sometimes he lay and tried to think of something to say to Serena while she ran on about a dinner they had been to and the people there. Mostly he pretended to fall asleep. None of it mattered; he didn't care that Tubby Bates was going to marry again or that Mertie Fuller was going to build in Connecticut, or that the

Junior League was going to hold a bazaar for Britain. They didn't say one thing in a year that mattered.

He wondered sometimes, if he lost his health how Serena would take it, but he shuddered at the idea. Serena would think of everything. She would see to nurses and diets and bed rest, and go on with her own life. If he lost his position and she lost her money, then she would get a position through this or that influential person who had known her father. She would make a success of it.

He tried, cruelly, to think of some point of vulnerability, but she was so safe from hurt. He had even tried hurting her, telling her some of these things, and she hadn't let herself be hurt. She had been tolerant and reasonable with him, but safely preoccupied. That was in the spring when she did over the downstairs.

Once he had looked up the word complacent, and it meant "serenely contented with oneself" . . . Serena! It bothered him to stand outside and study her. She was his wife; someone he had married to live his life with, whose life was to be part of his.

How had he fallen in love with her in the beginning? His mind had worn a groove through his thoughts back to that fall of his Senior year. He saw Serena driving her open car when she brought her cousin back to school. He had been sitting in the window in George Flenner's room. She was so beautiful he had stared. After he met her, they were always doing things together: playing badminton or tennis or golf or swimming. They had never talked much; they hadn't needed to. They had danced together and said they were made for each other.

They were married at the end of that summer, and he had hardly dared breathe for fear of jarring loose his happiness. He had taken the first good opening in engineering that located him in New York; it hadn't seemed much to do if she wanted to live there. For a year they had done things every minute: gone places, trips, crazy things that everybody didn't do; they were young and lucky and in love.

There had been little things to mar his happiness. Loving Serena hadn't been quite the ecstasy he had thought it would be. She was so . . . so reasonable about that. She called it being intelligent. She talked it all over with him. That was right and sense, of course, but Serena's way stripped it down to something, as Serena said, "something perfectly normal and natural," some masculine urge that the intelligent young woman of today understood. So did another kind of woman, too.

"We don't want children now, John. It's a mistake until all the adjustments to each other are made."

There were more adjustments now than there had been in the beginning. Not that he cared. He wasn't like some men who wanted a son or a daughter above everything. He wanted Serena; he wanted her to want him. A man and woman could hold all there was of life between them, couldn't they? He wasn't sure any more. Four years they had had together, and where had they come? What did they have?

He had wanted to love her tonight. To erase the sound of her voice with the nagging edge to it. Physically, he loved her as much as in the beginning, maybe more. Physically, wasn't that the way the text books put it? That was the way Serena had things divided: physically and mentally . . . damn these psychology courses in women's colleges that turned out their flocks of bright, knowing young women. They thought they knew everything about men, and they didn't know anything about human beings.

Burns had said something once. . . . He lay still trying to get back in his mind to that time. Then he remembered.

He must have been about fifteen that summer when Monty bought his own ranch and got his wife through a marriage bureau. Everyone in the valley knew about it.

One day they rode over to Monty's ranch. Monty had built a new cabin for his bride, and the corral was new, too. Everything looked neat and spruced up. A creek flowed through their land, and willows and aspens grew close to the cabin.

They came around the cabin wondering what Monty's bride would be like. Monty brought her out, and he was kind of fussed. She was too thin and pale to be good to look at, and her face looked as though she'd been crying.

"I'm sure glad you folks came by," Monty told them. "Thelma's been lonesome out here all by herself." Thelma smiled at them feebly, but when Burns said they'd stay for supper, she put on lipstick and rouge by the mirror over the washstand. By the time they left she was laughing and talking as gay as anything. She looked like a different woman, and Monty seemed proud of her.

They rode back in the dark, not talking much. The horses were anxious to get home and wanted to run all the way. They forded the creek just below Burns', and as they came up on the near bank Burns said, "Poor Monty, his wife don't feel it's worth while smiling just for him, not unless she's got company. She won't stay long out there alone with him."

Funny, he could remember now the sad, lonely feeling of the dark, with the water cold where it had splashed up on his ankles. They'd run the horses in, then, and he remembered how good and cheerful the cabin looked. It was a man's place, without any women around. A sudden fear had bothered him.

"Burns, you wouldn't get a wife like Monty, would you?"

He remembered Burns' big laugh. "No, boy, not that way. I wouldn't want any woman unless she wouldn't care whether we lived next to mountains or railroad tracks or whether there was another person in the world as long as there was us. That's love, and you don't find it very often." And Burns hadn't married.

He hadn't listened to what Serena was saying, but the sarcasm in her tone caught his ear.

"I know you're thrilled to be back here, but, after all, you want to remember that the rest aren't excited just because you used to spend all your summers here."

"I don't expect them to be. I didn't ask them on this trip, you'll remember. I had thought you might not be bored coming up here with me alone." He spoke in a low voice, so evenly his words sounded innocent enough.

He knocked his pipe out on a rock and busied

himself with covering the ashes with gravel. It was as near as they ever came to a quarrel. After all, there was nothing to quarrel about. You couldn't argue your wife into wanting to be alone with you. It made you out an ass, even in your own mind. But this business of not ever being able to explain things to Serena, to see alike, was intolerable.

"I think Victor and Walt got awfuly tired riding up here," Serena went on. "Don't let Burns go too far tomorrow, will you? We don't have to make any definite goal."

"Can't stop unless there's good feed for the horses," he grunted.

"Aren't you going to bed, John?"

"In a while." But the open spot on the rise of ground was too close in the dark. In his woolen socks he walked down from the knoll toward the creek.

Burns had banked the fire and rolled up beside it on a bed made of saddle blankets. The plain below the reef was still. At the end of the road, the creek glittered like coal. But the familiar sense of depression filled him.

The small pebbles hurt his feet. He stepped on a big stone close to the water, feeling the surface smooth under his feet. He listened to the sound of the stream until he could hear the people talking.

He reached in his pocket for his old collapsible drinking cup. The water was so cold it stung his throat. But it was good. Running water when it came down from the mountains was twice as good as any well water; it had more flavor. He rinsed the cup and threw the spray into the willows that edged the creek. Then he filled it again and padded softly up to the knoll.

He remembered when he had received that cup. It was his first summer up here. He had written in to his father to be sure and send him a drinking cup, and it had come the day they went to the Chinese Wall. He had wanted nothing more that day, nothing at all. That was a long time ago.

"Want a drink?" he said in a low voice to Serena.

"Thanks." Serena propped herself up on one elbow. She hadn't been asleep. Perhaps she was miserable, too. He sat on the edge of his bed waiting. If Serena said one word . . . but Serena handed back the cup and shrugged deeper into her blankets. He undressed and slid into his.

Once there was the fluttering sound of a bat flying in a blind, meaningless circle over their heads, and always the low gabble of the stream and the wind in the aspens. He held his breath to listen. Serena was asleep.

TUESDAY

4

THE bell came faintly from the steep hill above him, a sweet jingling sound, remote from the valley. All night the horses had hovered close to the camp, but with the first light they had been off up the mountain for new pastures. Now they were out of sight. John stood still trying to catch a glimpse of them. Burns' taunt was still in his ears.

"Think you still can, boy?" and Burns' slow grin.

"Why, you son of a gun!" he had answered softly, so as not to wake the others, and set off up the hill through the heavy dew. On other trips he had always gone for the horses while Burns cooked breakfast. He had learned to run like a goat up the mountainside. He could guess out their hiding places. He couldn't forget, but his wind wasn't what it used to be. The calves of his legs ached after even a short spurt. Soft he was, in more than the calves of his legs. He worked his way up the mountain more slowly.

The bell tinkled sweetly, mockingly, up above a clump of cedar. That was all rock back of the cedars; the horses wouldn't be there. He waited, listening. Funny how different a bell on the jingle horse sounded from a cowbell. There it was! They were more to the left.

He brushed through a cobweb spun between two fir trees and felt the wet clinging touch across his eyes. The earth breathed warmly in here where the fir trees grew close to the rocks. His feet sank into the spongy mat of old pine needles. There was no sound of a bell, but he had the sense of another living creature breathing somewhere near him. He had used to feel that sometimes up in the mountains. Perhaps it was the horses; Blaze was clever enough to stand still so the bell wouldn't jingle, just to fool him. He might be looking at him through some shelter, munching quietly with a shrewd horse grin on his lips. John started making noises to the horses.

"Here, Blaze, here, boy," speaking confidently. "Come on, boy!" Only the sound of his own breathing answered him. From down below he could catch the sound of voices. Someone shouted. They were getting up now.

"Here, boy." A chipmunk chattered and scittered

away from him. A camp robber swooped down from the reef with his unpleasant greedy cry, but there was no bell.

He didn't care if it took him all morning to find the horses. It was good to be way up here. When he got to that tree he would top the ridge and be able to look down on his old cabin.

"Do you want to camp around your own place tonight?" Burns had asked. And he had shaken his head.

"Too small. We'll go up by in the morning."

If he and Serena had come off up here alone they'd have gone out by themselves and stayed in his cabin a while. He walked slowly across the ridge.

There it was, just as he'd left it, looking smaller than ever from up here. The wooden strips that held the tar-paper roof on were as gray as the bark of an aspen tree. There were the antlers at the peak of the roof where he'd nailed them. There was the window he had cut himself, knocking so much of the chinking out he'd had to chink the whole side. The first piece of property he'd ever owned. He remembered his feeling when Burns said he could have it if he would pay the lease money; sixteen dollars a year paid to the National Forest.

He remembered the first time he had stayed in the cabin alone all night. He'd been twelve then; that was his first summer back from boarding school. He was full of Burns' stories of bears and mountain lions. He had gone to bed with every window closed and the door barred and been so scared he couldn't stretch out under the blanket; just huddled there, listening. A tree sawed against the cabin. Pack rats ran across the roof. An old jacket he had hung on a peg outside thumped against the window. It was so hot inside he was sweating. Then he was ashamed. He walked over to the door and threw it open. Out on the stoop he could see the stars, and hear the wind and the creek. There was nothing there but the night. He went back in and slept with the door to the cabin wide open. In the morning he had felt inches taller.

From up here he could see the fresh chinking between the logs. Burns looked the cabin over every so often and kept it up. He paid the lease every year; still sixteen dollars. He always would.

John heard a noise in the bushes and turned quickly. There was Blaze, munching a thistle, watching him with large bright eyes. He had caught a branch under the strap that held the bell so it didn't ring.

"Here, Blaze, here, boy." The horse stood still, waiting for him. He laid his hand on the horse's neck. There were the others, two of them still lying down. Flash whinnied.

He pulled himself up on Blaze's back, not too proud of the way he had to help himself up by the mane. He took the branch that held the bell for a whip, but Blaze was ready to go. John could feel the warm belly under his legs as he rode bareback down the hill behind the other horses.

"Hi there . . . you!" He might have been fourteen, sixteen, twenty. . . . "Hi-yi-ee" he called when he had the horses down on safe ground and had set them running in. He was Pickett charging, or Custer meeting the Indians, or the head of the Vigilantes sweeping down on the rustlers, just as he used to be.

"When do we eat?" he yelled at the top of his lungs, bringing the horses up within a few paces of the fire where they were all eating.

"I thought you'd gone on ahead to pick the next camp site, you were gone so long," Burns told him.

"John, you're wonderful!" Lizzie called out.

"That's what you brought us out to see, that act; I know!" Walt grinned. "Hurry up and I'll cook you some swell sourdoughs."

"John, turn your horse's head, just a little; now come toward me, fast; this'll make a wonderful movie. Vic, can you snap them as they run by?"

"I have them. They'll look like wild horses." Serena and Victor were intent on their cameras, and suddenly, John felt like a kid that has been showing off.

"Darndest thing, Burns, Blaze got a stick caught in the halter and bell so the bell didn't ring; that's why it took me so long," he muttered as he might have explained ten years ago.

They were late starting. They weren't used to rolling sleeping bags or helping to saddle horses, but they all wanted to help. Victor was better than Walt. "That's my Magyar ancestry," he explained with a smile.

John watched Burns out of the corner of his eye. Burns was loosening the whole pack again to show Vic and Walt how you did the diamond hitch. Burns' hat with the frayed band was pushed a little far back for equanimity. His cigarette had gone out. He never had liked taking dudes out, really.

"Let's start on," John said to Serena. "I want to show you the shack where I used to stay." He was pleased with her quick assent.

They rode up the trail through the fading green aspens that would be yellow when they came back in three weeks. It would be hot later in the day, but now a lazy warmth fell pleasantly on them. The tenseness and depression of the night before disappeared under it like a chill before the sun. Whenever his mind went back to last night, he stopped it. Slowly the pleasure of being here again grew in him. He looked at Serena. She grinned back. She had dismissed last night, or it had not seemed important to her.

"There she be!" he announced. "You don't see it until you're right on it."

They tied their horses to the old hitching bar he had nailed between two trees years ago. He unlocked the door with the key that was always on his key-ring, even though Serena had long ago pointed out the foolishness of carrying it.

"At last, you're using that key, John!" she teased.

"You see, it was worth carrying all these years, after all! I knew we'd come back," he retorted with mock gravity.

It was dark inside. He had forgotten how small the cabin really was; just one room and the tiny lean-to kitchen. He knocked the wooden buttons free and pushed back the windows. Now it was not so dark. You could just see to read lying on the bunks if you held your book the right way, he remembered. There were two bunks against the back wall; their mattresses, rolled into bundles, were strung from a crossbeam. The logs rose to ten feet at the ridgepole, but came five feet from the ground at the sides. They were a weathered color. He walked over to the stove and lifted the lid of the airtight. The wire handle that always felt as though it would come off, but never did, was more familiar to him than most handclasps. He looked around the small room with satisfaction.

"If we'd come alone we could have spent a week or two here."

"Darling, you overrate me as a camper."

"It's really just a place to store duffle, of course, but it's pretty complete," John said. He touched the handle of the fishing rod on the wall and glanced over the row of books on the shelf over the window: *Stalky and Co.;* a Latin grammar; a diary, half kept, as usual; *Kidnapped;* and then, right next to it, as though he had suddenly grown up, there were *A Farewell to Arms* and *All Quiet on the Western Front* and *Jurgen.* One summer he had thought *Jurgen* wonderful, he remembered, and the next it seemed stupid. He would have liked to sit down and look them over again.

It seemed stuffy in the cabin. Mice leavings littered the table around the gnawed candle. There was the chair he'd made himself out of aspen wood, with rawhide for the seat.

"This is the place you used to talk so much about.

I remember you wrote me from here. But your father must have been crazy to let you stay up here all alone. It's no wonder that you're moody sometimes."

"I don't know; I think it was good for me. Anyway, I liked it. The cabin's different, of course, when it's aired out and lived in. Let's go out on the porch and wait for the rest." He dragged the rawhide-covered chair out for her and lighted her cigarette. He felt a little shabby about the cabin, dismissing it so lightly. "It's a snug place when you really move in and live here. I came up the summer before we were married, remember? I didn't do much that time but think about you; what it was going to be like having you."

A pleased little smile flickered across Serena's firm mouth. "I remember Mother was so glad you were away then, because there were so many things to do about the wedding and you were always at the house wanting to do something with me."

John sucked on his pipe. "S'rena, what's happened to it? It's not the way I used to think it would be. It's too . . . well, it just doesn't mean enough to either of us."

"What do you mean, John? I don't see why you say that." Serena's voice was completely reasonable, the way it was when they discussed anything. She was looking directly at him. John found himself studying her, trying to let all those lines of face and head and body that he loved say more than she did, let them make up for . . . well, for what he missed. It was an old game. He had done it before they were married, but he hadn't admitted it then.

She was lovely to look at. He tried to let that be enough. Her soft chamois jerkin deepened the warm tan of her neck and matched the lighter lock of hair that twisted in with the rest. Without touching her hair, he knew how it felt in his fingers. Then the very things he loved about her made him angry.

"It's true, Serena. What do we really mean to each other? Last night, I came up the hill so eager to love you, feeling that everything was going to be different up here. And you started bargaining, worrying about these people you dragged along. You don't need me; you don't even understand what I'm driving at."

Her face lost its clear, serene expression. It was troubled. He looked away from her to the clean gray boles of the aspens that hid the trail. The others would be here any moment. He must say what he had to say, get it out between them, make it clear and then never try again. But it didn't go easily into words. He waited so long she spoke first.

"Of course, there are always adjustments to be made between two personalities."

He groaned to himself. She had said this before so many times. It was a cliché she had learned in college. It didn't mean anything.

"That's true of any marriage, but ours is certainly as successful a relationship as . . ."

He winced at the word "successful." It meant so much to Serena. Then it came to him: that was where she was vulnerable. She had to feel that everything she had to do with was "successful." In the midst of his own anger at their lives, he felt sorry for her. She didn't even feel any lack in their lives together.

"And as for last night, John, I was ready to love you; you got temperamental. . . ."

He broke in quickly, sorry for both of them. He spoke gently, "Forget about last night, S'rena. Maybe the fault is just mine. Maybe it's the way the world is that makes you hate to think your life might mean more and doesn't. Maybe it's something we can't do anything about."

But sometimes, lately, he had wondered if he loved Serena, and it was like looking down the sheer side of old Baldy. If you got down there you

65

couldn't get back up easily. A man didn't have to have his wife in love with him. There was plenty else in the world, and maybe he was just being childish; or was he one of the poor dumb fools that did?

He thought of Serena's life; of everything that made up her day, from golf with Lizzie, luncheon with someone else, some Junior League social work, dinner, the evening. She kept busy; she didn't have any space in it for needing him or knowing him. Maybe he was asking more of her than she had it in her to feel. He looked at her now. Here they were: a man and his wife, sitting on the porch of a one-room shack, an everlasting symbol of marriage, but they made it meaningless. He had wanted to bring her back here. Well, here she was, and he had never been more unhappy with her.

"Let's be frank about this, John." Serena broke in on his thoughts. "I've known you were put out ever since I asked Victor to come on this trip. That's what you're trying to say. But you're inconsistent. We've always said we were free human beings, each with his own interests and friends, and then when I am interested in someone—and not in the way you try to suggest, but because I feel that we might do something for him by showing him a part of this country that he might not see, a kind of expedition that's so American. . . ."

"Oh, pipe down, for heaven's sake, Serena!" John said in a low voice, as though he didn't want the cabin to hear them. He was a fool ever to talk to Serena. He walked down the path to look for the others.

"Hi!" Burns came around the bend, through the trees. "How's it look to you, boy?"

"Not bad," John answered. "If we make the springs by afternoon, we better push on, hadn't we?"

5

VICTOR and Serena were ahead, then Lizzie and Walt and Rose, and John and Burns came last, each with three pack horses. They had to go single file. The sun climbed higher into a sky that was one unvaried blue ceiling. Where it had been soft and light in the morning, it became bright and hard as plaster. The heat came up from the dry grass and the dust-laden sage. The horses' hides smelled hot.

To John, it was good. At home, wherever you went, you went fast: by plane if you went on business, or you paid extra and took a crack train that made record time, or you went by car if you went into town, or by the subway that shot you through a tunnel to your destination. There was never any time to jog slowly along until your thoughts jogged, too.

"We look like a Canterbury pilgrimage!" Lizzie said.

"I'll be the friar," Victor announced and surprised them.

"When would you read Chaucer?" Serena asked abruptly.

"I went to Oxford, you know," Victor explained. "But I would have read it in my own country, as far as that goes."

"You'd make a cunning Nun Prioress, Serena," Lizzie teased.

"Why not the Wyf of Bath?"

"You'd have to get five husbands in a hurry," Walt reminded her.

"Oh, well, I've only got four to go!" Serena retorted.

"Burns will think you mean it; or Rose, here," Walt warned her.

Rose shook her head. "Dudes always talk a lot of stuff. I worked at a dude ranch one summer," she said, calmly unperturbed by the shout that greeted her words.

They came up on the top of a high ridge and reined in their horses to look around. The ground was bare. There were no trees. Beyond they could see rocky peak after rocky peak, bare and austere in the sun of midmorning. At sunset these peaks would soften and take unto themselves color, but now they were stark and barren.

"Now I see why the 'Rocky' Mountains," Walt said.

"It seems odd that there is so little green vegetation, Burns," Victor commented.

"Those peaks are high," Burns answered.

"I hope we get out of this kind of country pretty soon," Serena said.

John was going to keep still. "I know you're thrilled to be back here, but, after all, you want to remember the rest aren't excited just because you used to spend all your summers here," Serena had said. Then, to save his soul he had to tell them about this place.

"This looks as though it had never seen anybody but trappers, but as a matter of fact, the Great North Trail went up this way. Thousands of people must have come over it on their way from Mexico to the Arctic Circle," he said quietly, but he remembered the excitement he used to feel when he stood here.

"I found a Roman coin here one summer with the head of the Emperor Hadrian on it. Must have been brought up here by some Indians that traded with Spaniards in Mexico."

"That's so; I'd almost forgotten that, John," Burns said, pushing his hat back and wiping his forehead.

Tuesday

"Here!" Victor marveled. "I was thinking on the ride up how free from habitation and people all these mountains are, that it was a rest not to have them covered with the burden of humanity. But that is not so, after all."

"They look as though they've had plenty of years without people since this was a trail, though," Walt commented.

"Long enough, all right," Burns said. For a moment, no one spoke. The horses pulled at their reins. One took a step toward some tattered remnant of green. A rock rabbit uttered a sudden piercing squeal and froze again into silent immobility. John tried, as always, to see a long caravan of primitive people trudging up over the rocks. For him this place was never still. He could almost hear their grunting talk.

Lizzie gave a little shudder of dread. "It isn't bad in summer when it's warm, but if it were cold you certainly would feel unloved up here."

"It makes you feel unimportant, all right. We're just one of the races that passed this way," Walt said, smiling.

"With our own little wars and exiles and tragedies," Victor finished.

"I don't like mountains unless they have some

trees," Serena said decisively, bringing them all down to the present, shutting out the ages past.

"We're dropping down soon, again," Burns said, riding on along the barely discernible trail. He stopped suddenly and called back to John, "Look here! Do you see something over the next divide?"

John rode up beside him. "I see what you mean; that whitish thread that might be a cloud or might be smoke. It's pretty faint for smoke."

"But it has a bluish tinge, and it's so damned dry," Burns worried.

"Wouldn't the lookout up on Goat's Peak get it if it were smoke?"

"Should. He might be away, fixing his telephone wires or something."

"Victor, bring your glasses up here," John called.

But under the powerful lens the white thread was a thin skim of cloud, standing out only because the plaster sky was so nakedly blue. The air rising from the rocks quivered. The smooth fabric of the air that should have been invisible showed itself made of wavering streamers. Each rider and horse stood out against the sky as though mounted on a block of wood and set against a painted background.

It was a relief, at first, to come down from the rocky ridge into a forest of lodgepole pines. Here the sun was broken by the tall reddish trunks into striped bars of green light. The shade rested their eyes, but it was no cooler. The heat sank into the thick duff around the base of the trees and gave up a warm resinous smell.

"I like that heavy pine scent," Victor said.

"I don't," Walt answered. "It makes me think of steam inhalations for youngsters with colds, all next winter."

They ate when they came to a shallow creek. Burns opened some cans of sauerkraut and told them to get clean flat stones from the brook. Sauerkraut and slices of bread and ham. Lizzie wrinkled her nose.

"It isn't fancy, but the sauerkraut'll quench your thirst," Burns told them. "We'll push right along, because if we have any luck we ought to get a fool hen up here at Deer Park. You might keep your stones, and we'll see how good shots you are."

They got back into the saddle reluctantly.

"I'd like to rest in the middle of the day and ride in the evening," Lizzie said, but Burns was out of hearing back of them.

"You know this could become an endurance test instead of a vacation," Walt muttered to John.

"We have to get on up to Deer Park where there's feed and water for the horses; anyway, Burns wants to go on over to the fire tower to make sure that

73

was just cloud we saw back there. He's an emergency fire-guard. It's beautiful in here, though," John said.

Walt grunted. "Even beauty can grow monotonous if it goes on forever. I'm so sleepy now I could go to sleep on my horse."

"Vic, aren't you glad you came now?" Serena asked as they rode along together.

Victor's smile lighted up his face and then left it sober again. "I can't help thinking how strange it is for me to be here. Out here I feel much farther from Europe than in New York, I mean aside from the geographical distance. This country is so still and empty it forces your own thoughts back on yourself. I was riding along just now, thinking that I should have gone over to England and stayed there, offered my medical services. Of course, at the time I came to America we didn't know that all of Europe was going to be on fire."

"But I'm glad you're here," Serena said. Their eyes met for an instant. Then the lead horse started into a trot, and the whole line kept pace, the pack horses lumbering heavily in the rear.

"I could certainly do with a smoke," Walt said.

"Better not. Burns is as nervous as a cat about the woods because they're so dry. I wish we could get one good day of rain," John said. "We could lie in camp a day, and the rain would freshen the woods." He thought to himself that back here he accepted Burns' authority as he used to when he was a boy. He'd forgotten how they used to ride for hours without talking. He felt the silence resting heavily on Serena and Walt and Lizzie. He began to whistle. Then he broke off. Why should he worry about how they liked this trip? That was Serena's worry.

They came out into Deer Park. Without warning, the tall pines gave way to an acre or so of green grassy land without trees. It might have been a New England meadow except for the aspens and fir trees edging it around, and the absence of white birches and a dry stone wall to mark its boundary.

"This is where the deer come," Burns told them. "Don't think I've ever been here without seeing one. Keep your eyes peeled. And there ought to be some fool hens. A grouse would go all right for dinner tonight, wouldn't it, with some rice."

They rode silently, watching. Once Burns gave a whistle and pointed to an area of matted grass where deer had lain.

John saw the grouse first and slid out of his saddle. He handed the rope of the pack horses to Rose and, taking careful aim, hurled his stone. There was a fluttering in the bushes. Victor threw his. They ran like bird dogs. Victor came back carrying the hen grouse. One leg was broken. He held her gently, stroking her nervous head. Her sharp, fear-bright eye looked out from under his hand.

"Ah, Vic, let me take her." Serena reached down for the bird.

"Whst!" Burns whistled softly, pointing off toward a clump of willows. Rose was running stealthily across the meadow. She hurled her rock like a boy. The grouse rose on ponderous, whirring wings and flew into a fir tree. The subdued brown feathers were bronze in the sunlight.

Burns hurled his rock without dismounting. The bird dropped out of the tree.

"Oh, don't do that! I can't stand to see them killed," Lizzie protested. Rose looked at her in surprise and then, as though suddenly self-conscious, she moved around the other side of her horse, tucking her shirt loosely into her jeans. "That's the cruelest thing I ever saw. I hate to have Walt go duck hunting, too." Lizzie went on.

"That's silly, Lizzie. You ought to come with us next fall after quail. You'd be crazy about it," Serena told her, cuddling the frightened bird on her arm.

"Now if we could get two more," Burns said, ig-

76

noring Lizzie altogether. "We ought to run on to some more."

"Here, Serena," John came over to take the grouse.

"No, let me keep her, John, till we get there. I love her."

John started to take the bird away. It was better to kill it now. Then he looked at the picture Serena made; her bronze hair only a shade lighter than the bird's feathers, the bird held gently against her chamois jerkin.

"The lady with the falcon," Victor said, as though reading the title of a painting. John turned back to his own horse. When they were riding again, he had to look back. There was something medieval about the procession they made, coming across the green, grassy place. But his eyes rested on Serena, sitting so straight in her saddle, with the bird held in her arm.

"Feel his heart, Vic," Serena pulled in her horse. Victor rode closer to her and felt the bird's breast. He nodded.

John was suddenly angry. It was as though they held something precious and living between them. He wished he had wrung the bird's neck in the beginning. The grouse he had in his saddlebag was dead.

77

Unless the Wind Turns

Watching for a brown feathered movement on the ground gave new point to their riding. The hot, still afternoon quickened with suspense. John rode off to the right once on a hunting foray of his own, finding it good to gallop ahead. Then he slowed down to a walk and dismounted, hunting in earnest for another bird. The others had crossed the park now and entered the timber again.

John came back with two more grouse. He used to be good at bagging birds, and he came back pleased with his success. He held the two up for them to see.

"Good boy; that's plenty," Burns said.

Serena and Victor still rode side by side, talking as they rode. John rode back with Rose. Serena should see, he thought childishly; he wouldn't bother her again on this trip. He looked at Rose critically, thinking of the greater reticence of female horses about their breasts than females of the human species. Rose had put her hair back into the everlasting curlers, as though, having shown herself to them once in the glory of curled hair, now she was interested only in being beautiful for Mike.

"You're a good shot!" Rose said. He smiled as he took back the lead rope of the pack horses.

He saw how this trip would be; it would go on day after day for three weeks this way, each day with its peculiar irritations and hitches. Why had he thought he would see more clearly back here in the mountains or that things would straighten out between Serena and himself? There was no magic in the mountains. When he was here before, he had brought no complicated problems. He had never thought of riding through the timber as monotonous, but it was, as Walt said. Of course, he was nothing but a kid before. He missed riding alongside of Burns. The whole trip was a mistake.

"If Mike gets out enough logs we're going to build three rooms right at the start," Rose said dreamily, just behind him.

"Oh! That'll be fine." He came out of his own thoughts. "Is he good at building cabins?"

"Mike? I'll say. He's built lots of cabins for other folks. I guess he's good at everything. He won the hundred-dollar purse at the Rodeo at the State Fair last August. That's what we bought our furniture with. Talk about a lucky one!"

"I should say. He must be quite a rider," John said with genuine enthusiasm. He wondered if Serena ever spoke of him with such pride.

When they came to Deer Creek, Burns stopped. "We'll camp here for the night. I'll go across from here to the fire tower on Goat's Peak and make sure about that smoke I thought I saw."

"How far is it, Burns?" Serena asked.

"Not more than three miles, but most of it's up. You have to go afoot. It's on that mountain; can you make out that little knob sticking out up there?"

Walt groaned, getting wearily out of his saddle. "Suits me. I'm ready to stop."

"May I go with you, Burns?" Victor asked. "I like climbing."

"Sure; come along. Rose, you can fix those grouse, can't you? I'll kill that one before I go, Serena."

Serena stroked the small brown head a moment. The hen dropped one purple wrinkled eyelid as though in foretaste of doom and then blinked it resolutely open again. John thought Serena would object, but instead she let Burns take it without a word, and John was oddly pleased.

6

IN the end, all the men went with Burns. Lizzie made elaborate preparations for acquiring a sun-tan without burning and stretched out in the sun on her sleeping bag. Rose took the grouse some distance from the camp to clean and pick them. Serena watched the men climbing toward the reef until they were out of sight. She wanted to go with them, but Lizzie wouldn't want to stay alone with Rose.

"There isn't any sign of smoke in the sky now," she reported to Lizzie.

"Oh, well, let them go," Lizzie said sleepily. "This is my idea of a pack trip, not moving every minute."

The horses were tied over in some aspens. They stamped restlessly because of the flies. The sound of their tails switching, flailing the leaves with thin strands, slashed the silence of the mountains into ribbons. And the brassy rasp of the grasshoppers pierced the stillness further in a ceaseless rain of pinpricks. Over everything the dry oven heat beat down upon the earth.

Serena sat down idly against a rock. Unpleasantness nagged at her mind. When she was with the others, doing something—even holding the grouse—it couldn't bother her, but now, left here to wait till the others came back, it crept in on her like a cold current in a warm pool. She hated being alone, anyway.

John had an uncanny power to ruin her pleasure, she thought resentfully. This morning at the cabin, saying their marriage didn't mean enough. . . . They had changed, that was all. She had changed, perhaps that was it; and John hadn't. John felt no responsibility to . . . to society. She did. His attitude toward Victor was an example. The fact that Victor was a refugee, an intelligent, cultured individual, driven out of his country, didn't seem to stir John as much as her interest in Victor had. She couldn't understand John. She picked up a handful of pine needles and let them run through her fingers.

John was angry at having Vic along, just as she'd said. He was jealous. Her mind squirmed away from the triteness of the pattern back to the night she had invited them all. Afterward, Vic had said to her in the hall, "You're very kind. I should like to go on your outing, but do you think I should? After all, I am an outsider."

"But we want you. We don't feel you are," she had said.

Then John had come out, and Victor had said to him, "I was just asking your wife if she doesn't feel that I should be an interloper on this trip you are planning."

"Oh," John had said stiffly. "Of course not, come along. The more the merrier." But Victor didn't know that he was annoyed. It didn't matter; Victor had come. "Of course, if you like him, take him along; that's the thing to do," John had said later, in that horrid sarcastic way of his.

His asking that girl to come was his idea of humor, a small vengeful kind of humor. Inviting Lizzie and Walt hadn't been premeditated. If she had to stop and think whether John would approve of everything she did, she wouldn't be living her own life at all. Hadn't she come West this summer just for John? She certainly hadn't wanted to; she would rather be at the Cape. She used to think that she and John liked so many of the same things, but they didn't, really. She wished Victor wouldn't try to think of them together.

"You're not as intense a people as I had thought," Victor had said this afternoon when they were riding along. "Take this trip; it's an easygoing, relaxing kind of holiday. It is more easy, I should think, for me to fall into this rhythm."

"Oh, this is really John's idea," she had told him.

"But you are John's wife. You like it, too."

She had shrugged. It seemed disloyal to say absolutely that she didn't. But it was true. The whole thing seemed stupidly aimless. They were going up to the Chinese Wall. And what was that but another granite reef, standing on end like a wall? John talked about it as though it were something tremendous: "the divide where all the waters on one side flow into the Gulf of Mexico and all the waters on the other side into the Pacific, kind of the ridgepole of the earth." And then they would ride back down again!

That was like John. She never knew what was going to be important to him. He had such funny obstinacies; like the time he insisted on chopping up those beech trees himself and lugging them all in or like, well, like this trip.

"Of course, John, if it's a matter of life or death to you . . . ," she had ended when he insisted on going here this summer.

"It is," he had said without smiling. "I believe it is."

"But why?"

Tuesday

"Wait till you get there. I hope you'll see for yourself."

One of these days, she would say to him, "Well, here we are; so what?" But this being off in the mountains *had* suddenly become important to her. Not because of the mountains or John, but because of Victor. Her eyes were on the fixed edge of the cliff. Her face was quiet, as secretive in expression as a forest animal's.

There was something offensive to her in the picture of a young married American woman in love with a foreigner. There were novels about that sort of thing; there was Betty Graves who married the ski instructor in Switzerland, there was that Wagner girl . . . but this was different. John was so . . . so immature; his life didn't touch hers at any point. That is . . . her thoughts drifted off into pictures of the last few days, of Victor . . . things he had said. . . . As though her thoughts pulled her to her feet, she stood up. Lizzie was asleep, and she went on down to find Rose.

"H'lo." Rose squatted on the ground picking feathers. "Want a feather for your hat? 'Course they're not pretty like the cock's."

Serena stuck it in her hair. "Can I help? It takes a long time, doesn't it?" Only two of the birds were done. Flies buzzed around Rose as she worked. She kept lifting her hands to shake them off.

"It shouldn't, but the smell makes me so darn sick."

"Oh, I'm sorry." Serena saw then how pale she looked. "Here, show me what to do."

"You don't need to. I've done plenty of birds, but I'm going to have a baby and things make me sick easy."

Serena was trying to pull the feathers off as Rose did it. "Should you ride, then?"

"Oh, sure. I'm not five months along. I thought you and the other girl would catch on, with me wearing my shirt out over my jeans."

"No, I didn't have any ideas." Serena didn't say that they hadn't looked at her very carefully.

"Mike's sure excited. He hopes it'll be a boy, so he can teach him to be a bronc peeler." The girl looked at Serena with a knowing smile. "I'd just as soon it'd be a girl, but I guess men get the biggest kick out of the first one's being a boy. After that they don't notice 'em so much, till they're big enough to tag after 'em."

They worked silently for a time under the noisy buzzing of the flies.

"I sure hope they don't find it's a fire. Fires are fierce this time of year. I don't guess they will.

Mike's up in the woods, and he'd have seen it and reported it in."

"I hope not, too. It would slow us up on our trip," Serena said.

"Say, the one you call Victor; did he really have to get out of Europe because of the Germans?"

"Oh, you mean Dr. Roth?" Serena said distantly. "Yes, he's a refugee."

Rose suspended work to think about it, holding the picked body of the partridge in her hands. "Gosh, that must be fierce to have to get out of where you've lived all your life. I know Mike wouldn't want to live any place else but Elkorn County if you paid him. Me neither."

"It's certainly hard," Serena said. Then, as though to John, she added, "That's why we were so glad to bring Dr. Roth on this pack trip, so he could see some of our mountain country." But her words sounded artificial and stilted even to herself.

"There, I'm glad that's all of 'em. Thanks for helping. We could've used a couple more, but these'll go good. Burns sure knows how to cook 'em, too."

Serena went back to Lizzie, who was combing her hair after her nap.

"Look at the tan I have already, S'rena; I ought to be beautiful by the time I get home."

"Say, Lizzie, that girl is pregnant!"

"Well! Women get that way, darling, didn't you know?" Lizzie turned her radio on, moving the dial slowly around.

But Serena was serious. "I know, but almost five months; would you ever guess it?"

"I hadn't, but that overhanging shirt of hers is pretty concealing. Darn it all, we've just missed the news!" There was a faint, incongruous sound of dinner music from an Eastern city.

Serena walked toward the trail to see if the men were coming. The streamer of cloud had swollen, and hung above the reef in a wide swathe. But it hardly resembled smoke, only that it didn't move. Didn't all clouds move if you watched them long enough? She wished Victor had stayed here. It looked like a hard trip up to the fire tower. John would enjoy it and never think that it might be too hard for someone else. John was really rather selfish, she thought critically. That was probably part of his immaturity.

When it got to be five o'clock Rose started a fire.

"If you girls want to help, we can have supper ready for the men when they get back here," Rose said.

"Look at the smoke this fire's making. Somebody'll see that and think it's a forest fire, won't they?" Lizzie asked.

"No, they know at the fire tower that we're in here with Burns," Rose said. "I wish Mike could get here for supper. He's a good camp cook, all right, but he didn't take any fancy grub in with him 'cause he's coming out as soon as he gets the logs out."

"Why didn't you go up with him in the first place?" Serena asked.

"I wanted to, but he didn't take any more stuff than he had to, and he thought it would be too hard on me. You know how men think you're made of glass when you're going to have a baby. But I didn't think how lonesome it was going to be." She smiled suddenly. Her thin freckled face, flushed from working over the fire, was attractive. Her body looked too slight to carry any secret of pregnancy.

"How old are you?" Serena asked abruptly.

"Eighteen. Mike's twenty."

"We can't do any more till they come, so we might as well sit down. This seems kinda like getting a church supper, all of us together, don't it?" Rose said.

"Exactly," Lizzie agreed. "So cozy."

In the afternoon light, the flames of the cook fire were pale and transparent. Lizzie's radio filled in the silence that stretched between the sound of the creek and the low swish of the aspens.

"Do I think it or are those trees moving more?" Lizzie asked.

"They always move. Burns says they make him think of nervous women. They don't me, though. I think they're pretty," Rose said. Then she frowned. "I hope the wind don't come up!"

"There they are!" Lizzie said. They heard a whistle up the trail. But only Victor appeared. He looked tired as he came across the hill.

"It's a fire, all right," he said. "From the fire tower, we could see the entire valley filled with smoke, as though it were down in a deep crevice. Burns got the forest ranger by phone. He ordered us all to the fire to fight it until they get men in there. Burns says for you to stay right here and perhaps give food to the trail crew when they come in. We have the emergency rations we took from the tower."

"What gulch is the fire in?" Rose asked. She looked sick again, Serena thought.

"I don't know," Victor said. "They talked about Big Timber."

"That's below where Mike's cutting," Rose said. One hand fingered the button at her neck. "I'd think he'd have seen it and sent in an alarm."

"Maybe he did," Serena suggested. "Maybe he's fighting the fire now with the others."

"Yes," Rose said. "He's probably doing that. I hope our logs are safe; the ones he's cut a-ready."

"It's funny we don't smell it," Lizzie said.

"There must be enough wind to carry it off the other way." Rose sniffed loudly. "You can smell it." She shoved the frying pan of grouse nearer to the fire.

"You're tired out, Victor. How about a highball?" Serena asked.

"That would be excellent." He smiled. "Part of the climb is difficult; the underbrush and fallen timber are so bad."

Serena made him a drink of Scotch and brook water in a tin drinking cup.

"Walt doesn't know anything about fighting fires," Lizzie fussed.

"Burns will know what to do," Victor said. "I must go right back. They sent me because they didn't want you to worry, and the ranger wants one of you to ride back to some station in the woods to get word to the fireguard. He's working on the trail somewhere around. It is about five miles. Burns says to make it in as rapid time as possible."

"I can go," Serena said quickly, "if Rose tells me how."

"Burns thought perhaps Rose . . ." Victor suggested.

"No, she shouldn't go," Serena said promptly. "I'll go."

"Serena, don't be crazy! It'll be pitch dark by the time you get back, and you'd get lost and we'd have to send out after you!" Lizzie protested.

Already the flames of their campfire had more color. It was still light, but the light had a bluish cast, as though it sickened.

"I'd better go. That's a bad trail along the mountain. You wouldn't know it, and you might get scared," Rose said.

"Don't worry, I wouldn't get scared," Serena said, stoutly. She took a childish pleasure in being brave before Victor.

Rose shook her head. "Burns meant me to go. I can make better time." She poured a cup of coffee and blew on it so she could drink it. "It's good we didn't let the horses out."

"But, do you think you should, Rose? The ride might hurt you," Serena protested.

"Riding don't ever hurt me. I'll ride to the hospital the day I have the baby, likely," she said with a sudden, unexpected grin.

"Seems as though we ought to hear a siren or a fire engine going by," Lizzie said. "Isn't it rotten luck to have a forest fire on our trip; Walt came out here for a rest."

"Don't worry about that. Your husbands are like boys," Victor said. "They are so eager for the excitement. Only Burns seems a little serious. He is worried, I think. He says some of the wood above the fire is virgin timber." Then, as an afterthought, he added, "I confess to sharing their excitement. Burning forests are too bad, but it is not like seeing homes where I have been a guest burned willfully. This means a waste, but it is not a tragedy."

"If the fire gets up to Bear Creek and burns Mike's logs, it will burn a home, all right!" Rose said. She had become less shy. She pulled on a leather jacket and buttoned it down the front, then, as quickly, unbuttoned it, letting it hang open. Out of one pocket she pulled a crumpled bandanna and tied it over her head.

"You haven't had anything to eat, Rose," Serena said.

"I'll take a piece of bread and butter and some of that chocolate to eat on the way."

"I still think I ought to go instead," Serena insisted.

"I know a short cut I couldn't ever tell you where to find. If the fire's bad enough to make Burns worry, the sooner they get men in there the better.

Look"—Rose turned to Victor—"you'll see Mike, 'cause he'll come down to help fight the fire; you tell him I'm with your party. I was going to surprise him; go into his camp and have supper waiting for him, see; but now you better tell him I'm here."

"I will. His name is Mike . . . ?"

"That's right. Mike Logan. You'll know him. He's a big tall fellow, kind of skinny. You folks better eat your supper; it's all ready to dish up. And maybe you better get stuff out to feed the trail crews when they come up. I'll be back to help."

They stood watching her mount, waving to her as she rode off.

"I wish I could have gone. It can't be good for her. She's pregnant, Victor!"

"Oh, I don't believe it will hurt her, a girl like that who is used to long rides. She could deliver her baby and be ready to ride again the same day, you know. I think I must eat quickly so I can return to the others," Victor said.

Serena served them as though she were serving a buffet supper at home. They sat on the ground with the tin plates on their knees.

"They fed upon the wing of a partridge and wild rice as they dwelt in the wilderness!" Lizzie declaimed with a bone in her hand.

"Only the rice isn't wild," Serena put in.

Tuesday

"The surroundings should supply that touch," Victor said. Lizzie leaned back so she could reach her radio.

"There! They ate their food in their fingers while they listened to music by the orchestra!"

"These birds are good; you ought to take some back to the boys and Burns," Serena said.

"Look!" Lizzie exclaimed.

The sky above the reef had a swollen pinkish tinge, as though it were tinted in water colors. They walked out into the opening to see it.

"It must be spreading!" Lizzie said. "Or else we can see it because it's getting dark. It shouldn't be dark yet; it's only five. Yesterday it was broad daylight until almost seven."

Victor changed into some heavier boots and put on a woolen shirt under his jacket. Serena filled a canvas bag with water for him.

"I think I'll take my camera along; ought to be able to get some good shots," Victor said. "Well, see you in the morning!"

Serena walked with him to the edge of the woods where a forester's blaze marked the trail.

"Be careful, Victor."

"Oh, I'm always careful." Victor smiled. "Didn't I leave Europe at the first sign of danger?"

"That was the only thing to do."

"Perhaps; sometimes, I think perhaps not. Don't worry about us; there's no great danger."

Serena turned back feeling that Victor had been about to say something more. She wished she had said something to show him she understood how he felt.

Across the hill, their fire that had seemed so big had burned down. Lizzie was collecting wood. A queer invisibility, neither dark nor light, veiled the clumps of sagebrush near by. Only the fringe of trees stood out darkly. It was still hot. It would be black as a pocket for Rose riding through the woods. She wished she had gone. She would like Victor and John, and Burns too, to know she had gone. It would be easier than waiting here. Fighting the fire would be easier, too. She thought, suddenly, of John's disgust when he saw Victor taking pictures at a fire. But, after all, why not?

"Say, Lazybones, do you know there isn't enough wood to keep the fire going very long?" Lizzie called to her.

Serena started after some. She found a broken limb of a tree and dragged it over to the fire. She took Burns' ax and set about chopping. The inaccurate blows of the ax resounded through the hot dusk. Beyond that and the horses' restless noises the place was uncomfortably quiet.

"I suppose we could let the fire die out," Lizzie said uncertainly.

"Oh, no; we ought to have some coffee hot to give any of the fire fighters. Don't you know, Rose said we ought to be ready to feed them," Serena said briskly, taking command of the situation.

"Serena!" Lizzie whispered suddenly. "Do you hear something?"

At the same moment, they saw the deer break out of the brush not more than three yards from them. As he stood with his head turned toward them, the reflection of their fire made his eyes two red flames and outlined his antlers with red. He stood a moment, then leaped away from them, and they heard him splashing through the brook.

Lizzie laughed nervously. "Whew, the Stag at Eve! I feel kind of like Beowulf in the forest primeval!"

"How about Robin Hood in the Rockies?" Serena laughed, but she knew what Lizzie meant. The queer light changed everything, and the deer had been running away. Even the aspens seemed to stand still to listen. She was listening, too, for the sound of the deer going through the brush on the other bank of the creek, but there was no sound. She walked softly down toward the creek. There was the deer, standing irresolute, in the middle of the stream.

"What's the matter?" Lizzie called.

"Nothing. The deer's still here." She watched it walk hesitatingly down the creek.

7

THE three men toiled through the woods carrying the heavy shovels and the hybrid mattock-axes, or Pulaskis, Burns had taken from the fire tower.

"You can smell it here, all right!" Walt said. "Look at the smoke!"

"Look at that!" John shouted. A moment ago the sky had been blue and placid behind the dark strokes of the trees; now it was covered over by a veil of smoke that darkened the day. A fallen log on the ground, a fir tree standing waist-high were half hidden in the smoke. Walt stumbled and fell once. John walked into a branch of a tree without seeing it. Burns plugged steadily through the woods. The resinous breath of pine and fallen leaves was swallowed up in the sharp smell of burned wood, pleasant at first, then fearful.

"It's over on the other hill, too, Burns!" John yelled in his excitement.

"Nope, it's just in the gulch. Better stop and get your wind." But when they stood still, the smell of the smoke came at them. A crow flew out of the tree in the gulch below them, black laboring wings fanning the air in warning. It uttered a single startled caw at their presence.

"You eat a bite here. We may be on the fire all night," Burns said. "Open up your stuff; I'll take a look around while I'm eating."

"We can wait; let's get there first," John said.

Burns shook his head. "Get something into you now."

"Nothing like eating while Rome burns!" Walt observed, opening the can of tinned beef. "These boots Burns had me take over there aren't exactly a perfect fit."

"Better than those riding boots you had, though."

They watched a darker cloud of smoke climb up the sky. They ate rapidly, brown bread and corned beef with a piece of cheese, and finished off with a swallow of water from their canteens.

Burns came back over the hill, his eyes reddened from smoke.

"It's still on the ground in the gulch. We've got a good chance of keeping it from climbing the hill if we can shut it in against that reef. How are you at digging?" He grinned at them. "I'm glad I sent

Victor back to the girls. They'll see the fireworks by now and get to worrying. Rose ought to get word to the fireguard in about an hour. There's some chance when it's low like this, but if a fire gets in the tops of the trees, you want to look out!"

They came onto the edge of fire so suddenly they weren't prepared for it.

"Holy Moses! I'd have walked into that if I hadn't seen Burns stop," Walt said.

At first, it seemed as though all the ground between the rocky sides of the draw smoldered. The thick duff gave up heavy smoke. Flakes of ashes rose slowly in the hot, still air and hung there motionless, as though supported by the heat. Here and there free flames licked at the base of a tree or devoured a low-growing cedar at one gulp with a startling show of force. The fire was low down, spreading by a slow creeping progress, but staying, for the most part, below a man's eyes where he could strike out at it to beat it out. The fire was deceptive in the extent of its spread, but it wasn't terrifying.

"That's not too bad a fire, is it, Burns?" John asked.

"Oh, 'bout an acre and a half to two acres, and it's been burning quite a while. You see, the bottom of this draw would be blind to the lookouts till the

Unless the Wind Turns

fire got a start." He dug up a shovelful of the red
smoldering duff.

"It throws enough heat!" Walt said.

"Not so much good timber in here; that's one
good thing," John said, looking at the low-growing
firs and underbrush, the dead snags of trees, burned
years before and still standing; a few thin-boled
aspens that had sprung up as suckers from old seed,
scattered through the burned area, the light gray of
their bark and the young green of their leaves pecu-
liarly pallid against the blackened snags.

Burns grunted. "Plenty of fuel up in there and
over there." He jerked his head toward the green firs
covering the sides of the draw above the rocky out-
croppings. "We'll start in here on the side hill and
dig a trench. Be sure you get down to the mineral
soil and dig it clean so the fire can't jump it. Here,
lemme show you!"

Walt felt himself puny trying to dig dirt under
Burns' eyes.

"Turn it more," Burns directed. Walt turned it,
but his shovel didn't cut far into the sandy soil. He
wondered how long the pigskin gloves he had worn
last year driving were going to last him at this job.

"Now keep that distance between you so you don't
hit each other with your shovels," Burns said.

John dug ahead, stepping on his shovel to force

102

it deeper. "Burns, this makes me think of the summer I got up here and you set me digging a hole for an out house, remember? I kinda kicked about it, and you said, 'When you're better at digging, you can have a better job.'" The boys laughed, but Burns only gave a grunt and nod. He walked through the heavy duff to the nearest snag that stood thirty feet high. His ax against the dead trunk struck out a flat, punky sound that reverberated through the woods. When the trunk fell into the burning duff, it strired up a shower of black and white ash.

The heat and smoke came at them. "Gosh, feel that heat!" Walt shouted. "I can feel it through the soles of my shoes even."

The burning duff came up to the ankles of their boots. Cinders landed on their shirts, singeing through the flannel. Sweat ran from their faces and down their backs. Walt had to stop to get his wind. He looked at John. It was tough for him, too.

Their shovels hit stone and came up empty. They struck roots, twisted like cables into the earth, and had to go at them with Pulaskis.

"It's the damned smoke!" Walt choked. "If there were more fire it wouldn't smoke so, would it?" He stopped to take a drink of water from his canteen.

"It's my eyes that get me," John shouted back,

looking away from the fire into the green shadow of the trees growing above the draw.

Burns watched a snag falling close to the trench. The small flames from the log reached out toward the trench, found no fuel and stood almost erect, like a snake seeking a place to strike, then coiled back on the log. He wiped his face.

"It's awful close in here," he muttered anxiously.

"D'you see it go back from the trench?" John yelled. A boyish hilarity was in his voice. He grabbed harder on his shovel and dug in again. "I bet you we get it stopped before the forest ranger ever gets here."

" 'Tisn't out yet," Burns shouted back.

"What? Can't hear you!" John yelled.

Burns shook his head. It was curiously hard to make yourself heard in the lowering atmosphere. They seemed shut in. Not the slightest current moved through the canyon. They breathed in the burned, smoky air, and it brought no relief to their lungs.

Walt stopped to take another drink from his canteen.

"Hey, John!" He couldn't make him hear. He waited to get more wind. "John! Got any aspirin?"

"Huh?"

"Aspirin!" He shrieked so loud the effort seemed to split his head.

John shook his head, not wasting breath to talk. He had to take his Pulaski to loosen the soil before he could get his shovel in. The smoke caught him full in the throat.

Burns felled another snag out in the midst of the burning ground. The sound of its fall was loud but not clear. It started no echoes. John noticed the quiet uneasily, a dead kind of quiet. That was because they were down here at the base of the draw. Since that crow, they hadn't heard or seen a bird or squirrel, or heard a single animal sound. Must've all cleared out because of the fire. The fire wasn't bad. They had it under control now except for watching it. He stepped back to dig in again.

A juniper close to the trench caught fire with a hideous, eager crackle. In an instant, the bush was a coral filagree. The juniper berries shriveled to black. John dumped a shovel of dirt on the burning bush, but the dirt slid off through the branches, leaving it smoldering. The aromatic smell of the cedar was so strong he could almost taste it between his teeth. It freshened the burned smoky air. He breathed it in. There was more than the smell of the cedar; there was fresh air. He felt it on his face. He glanced up and saw that the smoke clouds had shifted enough to show sky above. It was still blue, streaked with pink. It had been so dark in here he had thought it was already dusk. Then the smoke bellied out again, covering the sky.

Burns yelled. Couldn't hear what he said. His face in the firelight looked angry. Walt had noticed something was up. He had stopped shoveling.

The flames on the juniper bush brightened as though they were fanned. A breath of air had blown through the draw. The stifling cap that had pressed down on them lifted. Then John saw the flames that had crept up the length of a snag blow out at the broken top. A burning fragment fell to the ground. Another piece broke free, and seemed to sail up the slope. Burns yelled again.

The burning brand carried like a torch over into the green tamaracks and spruce. John sprang to put out the spot fire; but before he could reach it, there was a snap and crackle, and the flame traveled up the oozing, pitch-covered trunk of a green hemlock. The whole tree exploded into flame with a sudden, terrible roar.

"If a fire gets in the tops of the trees . . ." It was in the tops now.

The fire jumped from one tree to another. John saw it with his own eyes. It was climbing up the draw. What good was their trench? As useless as the

Maginot Line. If it kept spreading, it would be in thick timber. A hot wind, driving the fire ahead of it, blew past him. The dark, unburned trees above them swayed mournfully in the wind.

"God damn that wind!" John could hear Burns clearly enough now. His voice was hoarse. "Come on, boys!"

They followed Burns up the sandstone draw, finding footholes where they could, digging in with their fingers, pulling themselves up by the tough jack pines that grew in notches of the stone. What was Burns' idea? Branches snapped loudly, like the sound of his old .22 rifle, John thought. He looked back. The fire had crossed their silly trench. It no longer jumped; it rode on the wind.

"Spotting thick!" Burns grumbled. "Got to do what we can. John, go over there by that tree. Walt, work from here. I'll cover this part. Keep an eye out for Victor. He ought to be along. Harley'll be along, too. He's the ranger. It'll be a couple of hours before we get any fighters in here." Here above the fire they could talk without shouting; it seemed queer.

They fell to work without stopping to look when a new crackle exploded. The fire lit up the woods. The separate pops and crackles were gradually lost under the heavy roar.

"It's got away from us," Walt yelled, watching in horror as the flames traveled from one tree to another without waiting to burn down the trunk. But his voice was swallowed up in the roar. The hot wind came up the draw as though it were blowing through a chimney. He saw Burns yell, but he couldn't hear what he said. Burns was pointing. His face was distorted in a scowl and ludicrously blackened with smoke. He saw John nod back.

"It's crowning!" John shouted to Walt. "Look at her!" John's face showed only excitement. The red light of the fire fell on his face. He was yelling something back to Burns. Walt heard only the end of Burns' answer, ". . . too fast."

John was going some place; back down the draw. "Damn the smoke!" Walt muttered.

It was easier going back down. John let himself go and slid part way. Victor ought to be there by this time; the ranger, too. That would be two more. The duff was still red hot. Wisps of smoke spiraled up through the burned-over space. If the wind had only held off until they could get the snags down! Down here the roar sounded like a furnace fire with the door suddenly opened.

Victor and the ranger would be coming on the run when they heard that. John reached the trench they had dug. He looked back. The fire stood up like a wall at the top of the draw; the big trunks of the trees looked like kindling wood against the flames. He was panting so it hurt him to swallow. His mouth felt dry. His chest ached. Couldn't stop here.

He chafed at leaving the fire. He had to keep turning around to see how it had spread. Burns said they must keep together. Victor might not know which way to go when he saw the fire. Then he saw him and swore.

Victor had climbed a rock and was taking careful aim at the fire with his camera, as intent as though he'd come out for that purpose. John came almost up to him.

"Great show, isn't it?" His voice was so hoarse from shouting above the roar the effect of sarcasm was lost.

Victor smiled. "I don't know that it'll take, but it's a tremendous sight." Quickly and efficiently he pocketed the Leica. "I was wondering how I'd go about finding you."

"Girls all right?" John asked, ignoring the camera episode.

"Entirely. Rose left before I did to tell the fire-guard. I had no idea from down there that it was such a fire."

"It wasn't until the wind started up. Damnedest thing you ever saw. Girls scared at being left alone?"

Victor shook his head. "I cannot imagine Serena being afraid."

"She isn't often," John admitted. "Don't know about Lizzie."

Victor shook his head. "Both quite gay. They had dinner ready. I stopped long enough to have a piece of partridge and a highball! I regret to mention that." He laughed.

"We've got to get back there quick," John said. "Burns and Walt are up there alone." He turned and jogged back over the trail, stopping only to point out the trench. "We thought we had it stopped in here at first. Did have until the wind struck." The roar was growing; he gave up talking.

They could see the fire spreading. John wondered how many miles a minute a fire could cover. It had spread out both sides of the draw, fanwise. No good now to climb up the side. They'd have to go back farther and work up through the windfall.

Halfway up through the brush, the forest ranger caught up with them. He was a tall, lean man who climbed without being winded, in spite of carrying a heavy pack. He told them he was Harley, the assistant ranger, and asked how far the fire had gone.

"It must be up in Bear Creek by now," he muttered. "That's heavy fuel." Then he took the lead, setting such a pace that John and Walt had trouble keeping him in sight. But his words stayed with John.

Bear Creek. . . . So many of these names were familiar from other summers. What was it about Bear Creek?

"Mike says it's so dry up at Bear Creek there ain't any creek at all, hardly," Rose had said yesterday. "If Mike gets out enough logs, we're going to build three rooms right at the start," Rose had said today, riding along behind him, and he had wondered if Serena ever sounded as proud of him as Rose did of her Mike.

Where was Mike now? Why hadn't he seen the fire and reported it? Or couldn't he see it from there?

He plunged ahead recklessly to catch up with the ranger.

"Hey!" he yelled. Against the roar, the ranger didn't hear him until he was beside him. "There's a man up in Bear Creek, logging. Mike; don't know his last name. A girl we brought along with us is on her way to see him." The smoke got him when he tried to talk.

The ranger's face was grave and unrevealing.

"Mike Logan; I know him. He was in at the station a few weeks ago and got a timber sale permit."

In the minute's silence the roar came closer. It seemed almost upon them. The sky was completely covered with smoke and flame.

"We'll find Burns first," Harley said, and set out again. John waited until Victor caught up with him.

"Rose's husband is up there," he shouted, nodding toward the fire. "Harley thinks the fire's there already!"

"Wouldn't he see it coming and get out?" Victor asked.

"Maybe he couldn't." John went on, but every step was different now. He had never seen Mike, but now he became someone he knew. He watched a tree across a gorge turn to writhing flame in half a second, and the flames leap on to the next. As far as he could see, the forest was on fire. They had to watch for burning firebrands. Limbs of trees fell only a little way off. He felt the heat increase until his skin under his shirt seemed burning. He stopped and took a drink from his canteen, shaking it to see how full it was. He soaked a corner of his handkerchief and wet his eyes with it. He wiped back the sweat and grime around his lips. He could taste the dried sweat and the salt smarted on his cracked and blistered lips. God Almighty, what would it be like to burn to death!

Tuesday

He saw Burns and Walt, small black figures against the gigantic flames. He couldn't wait. He plunged ahead of Harley.

"Burns! Mike . . . Rose's Mike is up at Bear Creek." He stopped. He could tell by Burns' face that he remembered; that he had been thinking about just that.

8

"WHAT could four men do against a fire like that?" Lizzie asked in exasperation. "You can see that it's growing bigger all the time. Why don't they come back?"

"I don't believe they can come back until they get men in to fight it; you can't just walk off and leave a fire, but the crew ought to come soon," Serena said.

The two girls stood on a ridge above the open park where they were camped. To the north of them, the whole sky was red. They could see the fresh flames deepening the color, black smoke muddying the brightness, spreading it out over the whole sky till it seemed like evening.

"Listen to that!" Serena said.

They could hear the roar, faint but unmistakable, as deep as though it came from the fiery center of the universe. The horses were squealing and stamping in fear.

"I wonder if we ought to untie them," Serena worried.

"They might go home. We better keep them tied," Lizzie said. "We might as well go back and wait ourselves. There's nothing we can do."

They walked back down the hill to the campfire. By tacit consent, they stayed close together. They kept talking, pushing back the silence and loneliness of the mountains.

"I shouldn't think they'd need to send anyone to tell the fireguard. I should think they could see it for miles around. Everyone in that little town ought to be able to see it and come right out here to fight it," Serena burst out.

"You think the boys are all right, don't you, Serena?"

"Oh, yes, I think so. If they can't stop it, they'll just have to get out of its way and let it burn. I don't see how they can stop it now. I wonder if I could get a picture of that sky. Vic will, I guess."

"I bet he thinks he might as well be back in Europe," Lizzie speculated.

"Why, of course he doesn't, Lizzie."

"I mean being burned out and having to fight a fire."

"Why, there's no similarity at all. A forest fire is just a . . . a catastrophe. It isn't a tragedy."

Lizzie laughed. "Serena, you'd argue anywhere."

"Well, that's right." Serena hated to be laughed at. "Don't you remember Dr. Biggs lecturing on tragedy and saying that if you went along the street and a brick fell on you and killed you, that was a catastrophe; but if you were a contractor and one of your bricklayers whom you had mistreated dropped that brick, that was a tragedy?" Serena's voice unconsciously became didactic.

"Oh, Serena, for heaven's sake! I don't get that at all. Biggsy was a lame brain, I always thought. Why is the invasion of Vienna a tragedy then?"

"Why, because the handwriting was on the wall but the Viennese didn't read it. Vic says now that he looks back, he had plenty of warnings; but it's part of his temperament, of the Viennese temperament I suppose, to be easygoing and love living at the moment. One of his colleagues turned out to be a Nazi, just waiting to see Hitler come in.

A silence grew between them, thought on thought.

"Walt says he thinks it's hard on him to get so little money. I mean he's held an important position, obviously, and now he's just a lab worker. There are plenty of positions out of New York, but so many states have passed laws to keep out any refugee doctors."

"That's like John's attitude," Serena said. "I don't see how people can feel that way. Suppose they were refugees themselves!"

"Oh, there's a point. Walt said these Europeans have other ideas and ethics. But there are all kinds, of course."

"I hate that attitude," Serena said hotly. "That lumps them all in a mass and disregards the individual altogether. There's someone!"

A dozen men came across the brook, splashing carelessly through the water. In overalls and work shirts they looked like any group of farmers, except for a fancy belt on one, a bright bandanna on another, and the wide-brimmed hats they all wore.

"Hello," Serena said. "Where's Rose? The girl who took word down to you?"

"We didn't see any girl. The fireguard over to the ranger's station called in at the Benton ranch and told us to get over here to the fire. We're the closest ranch. They'll bring the fire crew in on trucks."

"Whereabouts is the fire now?" another of them asked.

"Can't you see it?" Lizzie asked with indignation.

The man laughed. "Sure I see the fireworks, lady, but that don't tell me just where it's at."

"I can't tell you that exactly, but I can show you where to go in to take the trail. Will you have some coffee and bread and butter or have you had your supper?" Serena asked.

"Did we? Say, Heine, did we? I forget." The men's guffaws were a strange relief in the silent woods. The men were younger and better looking than they had seemed at first.

"Sure we've had our supper, lady, but you can always feed fire fighters."

When the men left, the girls listened as long as they could hear any sound of them going up the trail; then the night was quiet again, and the roaring of the fire came closer.

"Maybe Rose'll stay down there at the ranger's station," Lizzie suggested.

"She wouldn't do that. She wants to see her husband too much."

They both heard the horses at the same time. "Rose!" Serena called sharply.

The man's voice answered them as he rode into the firelight. Rose came behind him on her horse. He introduced himself as Jackson, the district forest ranger.

"This girl's pretty tired," he said briefly. "I overtook her on the way back. We'll have plenty of men in here during the night. Don't worry. Harley is already in there by this time, and some men from Benton's ranch. We'll have to make our base camp for the crews just below here. This is far as the trucks can get. Maybe you better take turns down there at the stream to show the first trucks with the CCC boys where to go." The ranger tied his horse near the others and then came back to say to Rose, "Don't you worry any more, Rose; we'll be in there with him."

Rose nodded. A faint smile showed for a moment on her tired face.

"You're dead, aren't you?" Lizzie asked gently. "You didn't eat anything before you left either."

The girl's face looked pinched in the firelight.

"I'll be all right. I rode fast. I guess I never did make any better time. Do you know whether Mike's with Burns and them?"

"We haven't seen any of them since Victor left," Serena told her.

"It looks as though the fire were spreading over that way," Rose said indecisively, as though waiting for them to contradict her. "I can't make out why Mike didn't send in a report."

"The fire's getting down nearer this way, if you

ask me," Lizzie said cheerfully. "Sit down, and we'll get you something to eat."

Rose sat by the fire. She held the big tin cup in both hands. The bandanna had slipped off her head and lay like a scarf around her neck. Her eyes watched the sky. But she wouldn't eat.

"Honest, I don't want anything. I've got a pain in my stomick. I rode pretty fast for that trail."

"You don't think it hurt you?" Serena asked.

Rose shook her head. Lizzie put on more wood. Serena dragged her bed roll over near the fire.

"Here, you curl up and go to sleep."

Rose shook her head. "I can't sleep till I know about Mike. I'll lie down, though. Pretty soon we've got to go down to the creek to show them where to go. This is a heck of a place to try to get trucks into."

"Was it a hard ride?" Serena asked.

Rose shrugged her shoulders. "It was smoky the whole way. The horse kept stumbling. I guess the funny light in the sky and the smell of smoke made her nervous."

"Do you often have forest fires up here?" Lizzie asked.

"Sure, there's usually a forest fire somewheres in a dry summer, but they get 'em stopped quick. The ranger that came up with me says he wouldn't be surprised if this was a bad one, it's so dry. We could feel the wind picking up, too. That's bad."

A zooming sound began, faintly but distinctly, beyond the rim of the mountains. Serena stopped in the middle of a sentence.

"That's a scouting plane," Rose said. "I'm sure glad to hear it."

Suddenly the plane broke through the smoke clouds and passed low over their heads on its way up the canyon. The deep roar of the engine shut out for a moment the wind back of the aspens, and the creek and the unearthly roar of the fire.

"It seems like a war, almost, doesn't it?" Lizzie said. "I wonder if we could get anything on the radio." She lay down on the ground, turning the dial of her radio. "Lots of interference. . . . It's the fire, I guess."

"Turn it off, Lizzie!" Serena complained.

"I'd like to get some war news. We haven't heard a word since yesterday."

Through the confused noises a voice came clearly from some near-by local station.

"What is conjectured to be a very serious man-caused fire has broken out on the Deer Creek watershed, south fork. It is spreading rapidly up Bear Creek drainage. A scouting plane is already on its way to pick up a ranger to scout fire before dark this evening."

Lizzie snapped off the radio. There was again the overwhelming stillness of the mountains. Serena poured the grounds of the coffee on the fire, and the sharp sissing noise reproached Lizzie.

"You see, it is spreading," Rose said.

"Oh, just a little, probably," Serena answered quickly.

"I wish the boys would come, and Mike with them," Lizzie fussed.

"It's quarter of eight," Serena announced. She and Lizzie unrolled their sleeping bags near Rose. Last night they had avoided her, but tonight they wanted to keep near together.

"We might as well make ourselves comfortable," Lizzie remarked. Serena offered Rose a cigarette and was surprised when she accepted it. The glowing end was bright in the darkness. It was funny the way everything they touched or used seemed linked up with fire. She stamped her cigarette out.

"I forgot. John said we mustn't smoke in the woods while they were so dry."

Rose watched the smoke of her cigarette. "It don't matter now. Couldn't be a much worse fire than that."

Her tone of voice bothered Serena. She spoke

quickly to say something. "What do you suppose makes them think the fire was caused by a man?"

"The fireguard thinks it was some camper. There were a couple of men back in the mountains. Not Mike!" she added quickly. "He's terrible careful of fire."

"Is that the trucks?" Lizzie asked. They strained to hear, but there was only the sound of the brook and the roar of the fire.

"I'll go down there anyway," Rose said.

"I'll go with you," Serena offered.

"Say, I'm not staying here alone, don't think," Lizzie objected.

"Somebody better stay by the fire," Rose said. She had become the head of the party.

"Oh, I'll stay, if you aren't too long getting back," Lizzie gave in.

Together, Rose and Serena went through the woods. There was enough illumination from the sky to throw a queer reddish light on all the trees. A dead branch in the trail crackled with a sudden explosive sound. Serena looked behind her quickly.

"Gosh, I got cramps bad," Rose said.

"Didn't they stop when you were lying down?" Serena asked anxiously.

"Not much; they're bad ones."

"You don't think you're going to have a miscarriage, do you?"

"No, there's no danger when you get along this far. I'll feel O.K. when I know where Mike is."

"He's all right, I'm sure," Serena encouraged her. "He knows the woods, and he couldn't get lost or— or anything."

Rose kicked at the leaves on the path in front of her. "Burns says no one knows the woods in a forest fire. I've heard him say folks get so scared they just run wild, kinda. Smell the smoke! You'll smell that way down in Sweet Springs for a week, even after the fire's out."

At the creek, where the trail widened out, they sat down to wait.

"There's the Hooligans! That's what we call the C's 'cause of their crazy hats," Rose said. She waded through the brook to the opposite side. Suddenly the powerful yellow light from the truck cut through the woods and across the creek. It struck full on Rose in the middle of the trail, her face pale and small, her hair hanging in stiff blobs in her neck, her jeans wet up to the knee. She looked like a child except for the slight burgeoning of her body that was apparent as she stood in the headlights.

The green forest service truck filled with CCC boys roared to a stop. Rose ran up to the driver, pointing toward the other bank. Then she went ahead again through the ford. The truck slid cautiously down the bank into the innocent-looking stream. Water splashed white in front of the headlights and churned under the wheels. On the bank, the truck had looked big and powerful enough to span the creek at one charge, but in the water it seemed smaller, and a little absurd. In the beam from the lights, the rocks and boulders were gigantic, the pools twice as deep, the trees along the creek towering above them. The truck lurched wildly. The boys held on, yelling and joking like a crowd of small boys. "Ride 'em, cowboy!" one voice louder than the others sang out.

"Hold 'er, Gus, she's abucking!" It was somehow exciting and hilarious. Serena laughed at them. Rose watched soberly.

The truck stopped. The wheels still turned like mill wheels, the water poured over their spokes, but the truck advanced not at all. The driver shook his head and called back to the boys. They piled out, jumping over the sides of the truck into the stream. Watching them push, it seemed to Serena as though they could lift the truck bodily and carry it over. In the queer glare of light from the headlights and the fire-shot sky, the boys were no longer the lazy-seeming CCC boys she saw along the highways going through the motions of shoveling or digging; they looked like heroic figures in some gigantic mural. They shouted when the truck pulled itself up the other bank, scraping against the bushes as it went.

"The rest won't have any trouble following their tracks," Rose said; "we can go back up."

The girls gave the crew coffee and bread before they took their packs and went on into the fire, laughing and joking as though they were going to a ball game.

"Charming to have a camp for fire fighters just next to you!" Lizzie said. "Do you think we should move further up the stream?"

"They won't do any harm," Rose said. "I've cooked for fire fighters plenty of times. They're so dead when they come off'n the fire all they want to do is to eat and sleep."

"Oh, I didn't mean that!" Lizzie said in annoyance.

Serena persuaded Rose to lie down again on her sleeping bag. She and Lizzie washed the dozen tin cups that were all they had. Before they were through another truckload arrived. They could hear the men shouting as they crossed the stream.

And all through the night the trucks kept moving

up. The girls didn't bother with washing cups any longer.

They heard another truck grinding through the water, climbing the bank.

"That's the seventeenth truckload," Lizzie said; "I've kept count."

"Nineteenth! You must have gone to sleep and lost count," Serena said.

The entire sweep of sky from the dark rim of low mountain reef across to the snow-topped peak was colored red.

"It's gone way around the edge!" Lizzie whispered so as not to wake Rose. "They'll never get it stopped."

"You're right, Lizzie, about this seeming like a war," Serena murmured. "You know, you read about the truckloads of soldiers going through those towns in Europe all night, moving up to the front line. I suppose the women lie in bed and count the trucks and wait the way we've been doing. Sometimes, I'd give anything to be over there helping some way."

"Oh, Serena, you're crazy. We're lucky to be here," Lizzie said softly. "Why, you sound like a child craving excitement."

"No, it isn't excitement I crave, but I'm not sure we are lucky. And the war work we do! You know it's so much busy work. It may be some good to the people in England, but it's no good to us. It doesn't take anything of us, ourselves. The people over there have come to grips with something and know that they can take it. We don't know that; we don't know whether we have actual courage or not. We don't even know what we believe in."

"Why, Serena Davis, we know we believe in democracy, I should hope, and the right of the individual, all that sort of thing," Lizzie forgot to whisper.

Serena lay with her head propped on her arm, staring at the harshly colored sky.

"Yes, of course, but we don't know how much we'd do to prove it. You don't know what you believe in until you've had to give up something for it, do you?"

Lizzie laughed. "I'm glad John and Walt can't hear us. We sound as though we were back in school. I haven't talked, you know, about what you believe in for years."

"That's it. We don't. We just keep busy."

"Oh, I don't know. Walt reads aloud a lot. Books like *Union Now* and *Where Do We Go from Here,* books that make you think. And I go to the League's Current Opinion Group and that course of lectures at the College Club."

"That's what I mean. And you think how smart somebody looked or how somebody must have more brains than you ever gave him credit for because of the way he talked, or you don't read another chapter because Walt wants to stop now and love you and it's late anyway."

"Why, Serena!"

"That's the way it is, though," Serena said to the night, gloomily. "John thinks the answer to life is my wanting to love him more! Women in England and Europe, even in Germany, lots of them, must know they're living as people never lived before; they must know what they believe in or don't believe in, no matter what they're suffering or doing without or what they've lost. We don't. All the war means to us is heavier taxes."

"The trouble with you, Serena, is that you're not busy enough. All the rest of us your age have children, and we're thankful our children are safe over here."

"Everybody thinks having children is the answer and being so busy with them you don't have time to worry about things. When I have a child, I'll know first whether I'm really in love with its father or just married to him."

"Honestly, Serena, I never heard you talk like this before!"

Another truck labored up the bank with unusual clatter.

"That's the cook truck," Rose said.

"Oh, you're awake. How d'you feel?" Serena asked.

"I guess the baby didn't think much of the ride. He's twisting around inside of me. Wait'll I get him out. I'll pay him back with the spankings I'll give him!" she said in an attempt at humor.

Serena lighted a cigarette. Childbearing interested her in books, but not in life.

Rose rolled wretchedly to the other side. She looked ghostly in the red light from the sky, but then they all looked unreal.

"Why don't you take your curlers off? Aren't they uncomfortable to lie on?" Serena couldn't resist suggesting.

"I suppose I might as well. Mike'll have his mind on the fire and won't know whether my hair's curled or not after fighting the fire." She sat up and unrolled the metal clasps.

"Here, let me comb them out for you." Serena was amazed at herself.

Rose proffered a bright pink comb from the pocket of her jeans. "My hair needs washing, but there wasn't any good chance at Burns' place, and before that we was living in a tourist cabin. We know the folks that own it, and the season's over, so they let us use a cabin free. Anyway, I guess your hair always gets limp when you're having a baby."

Serena combed out the tight corkscrews into a soft curl. "There!"

Rose felt her hair experimentally.

"Say, you're good. Did you ever do beauty work?"

"No," Serena said, thinking what a good story this would make when she got home, but she was oddly pleased at the same time.

Rose lay back on her bed. "Honest to God! I never had such cramps."

Serena brought her some aspirin. "Try to sleep and you'll feel better."

"Can't you sleep, too?"

"I feel wide-awake. I will after a while," Serena said.

But she must have slept. When she woke, the others were asleep. The fire had burned out. It was quarter of three, but the sky was so shrouded in a yellowish pall of smoke and flame it gave no sign of morning. The flames reached up into the sky now. It was growing worse. The horses moved uneasily or hungrily over in the bushes. The hot wind stirred the aspens near them. The roar still came intermittently.

Serena walked up on the hill. The sky was more

brilliant up here, but it was frightening, too. The roar and a terrifying dryness came closer. How could the men stand to be over there, right in it?

The dry grass seemed to utter a sound. Then she saw a rabbit leaping past, its eyes, like the deer's, red with the firelight. All the animals must be moving out. They should be, too. John would love being in the thick of it, of course, he and Burns. Vic and Walt wouldn't want to leave them. Resentment rose in her against John.

She shouldn't have said that to Lizzie about being in love with your husband. Lizzie would tell Walt, and they would discuss whether she and John were in love. Rose must have heard her, too. But she didn't care. She meant it. She wasn't sure she did love John. She hadn't had enough courage to face that until tonight.

The hot wind passed by her with the choking smell of smoke heavy on its breath. The pine tree where she stood moved restlessly, as though it were drawn toward the fiery beauty of the trees beyond the reef.

While she watched, she saw a flaming brand ride through the air like a comet and land in an unburned clump of darkness. So immediate was the crackling flare of fire that she cried out and her own voice startled her.

Tuesday

In the queer lowering sky came the sound of a plane. It passed low over her head, on over the flaming forest. It must be the scouting plane, back again, but there was something ominous about its sound. In Europe, the plane would be a bomber spreading fire, she thought; killing people, a woman like her, just as she had met someone who stirred her, whom she might love. How hopeless and horrible to be cut off suddenly like that! She mustn't waste time. She must tell John as soon as he came back how she felt. It was better to tell him the truth. All the way back down the hill she thought of the words she would use.

"Did you see anyone from the fire?" Rose asked as she was near enough.

"No, I didn't see anyone. I just went up to the ridge. How are you?"

"She's not very good," Lizzie said. "I built up the fire to make her some tea. It takes forever to boil a cup of water over this fire."

"The fire's over to the right more, if anything," Serena began, "but it's burning just over the reef up there."

Rose caught her breath sharply. "Then it's way up toward Bear Creek, where Mike is." She buried her face with a kind of groan.

"Come over and see what you think about the

horses, Serena." Lizzie drew Serena out of hearing distance.

"Serena, I think she's in labor; she's having such steady pain. She's probably going to have a miscarriage."

"Good Lord, Lizzie. Do you know what to do? I don't."

Lizzie looked dubious. "We ought to try to get Walt or Victor. I thought we should go over to the camp and ask them to get word in."

The two girls stared at each other helplessly.

"It won't live if it's less than five months, will it?" Serena asked.

"Of course not."

"Did she say anything about it?"

"No, but she kept moaning every now and then. That's what woke me up. I thought it might be an appendix, but she's had that out. I asked her."

Lizzie went on over to the fire camp, and Serena went back to sit with Rose and wait.

9

"WHAT d'you think, Harley?" Burns asked.

The forest ranger lifted his hat and settled it again on his sweating forehead.

"We'll climb up there and see how it looks. Jackson is down with the crew." Harley went ahead through the burned duff, seeming not to turn from the awful heat as the others did. Walt had to keep watching the fire to make sure that it still burned away from them up the hill. It was moving faster, all the time with a louder roar. What if it backtracked? Burns stopped to put out a creeping fire burning along the ground from some flying spark.

"Could they get in there by plane, Burns?" John shouted.

"A plane couldn't tell much if the fire's already there. They can't send out another till daylight anyway."

It was hard climbing up the rocky side, but it rose

out of an old burn where there was no green fuel. The rock was hot and scarred black in places.

"Oughta be able to see something when we get up here," John muttered, leaning down to give Walt a hand.

But as far as they could see, the woods were on fire. On up to the top of the pass, way up and over to the side, there was still green stuff. Their smarting eyes sought it quickly, but the fire was moving with a greedy roar. It would be there before they could reach it.

Burns and the ranger stood staring for a long minute. They walked out on a ledge where they could see the whole gulch. Walt and John and Victor waited. Walt was coughing from the smoke. Victor tried an experimental camera shot at the fire. The camera itself was so hot he passed it for John to feel.

"We've got a grandstand seat, all right," Walt muttered.

Across the gorge the fire reared a solid wall of moving flame a hundred and fifty feet high. Brands were traveling a quarter of a mile ahead of the fire. The wind carried them like autumn leaves before it.

"If the wind would die down," Victor said, "but

blowing like this it seems foolhardy to risk going deeper."

"Maybe some of that fresh crew ought to go for Mike," Walt said. "Did you see how fast they worked at trenching?"

"They need 'em on the fire line. If anyone goes in for Mike, it'll have to be us," Burns answered.

The wall of flame lighted up the woods as far as they could see. It was bright enough to read by. It gave their faces unexpected high lights, touching off the black smoke streaks, polished by sweat, and their bloodshot eyes. Victor's hair looked light against his skin. John's teeth shone like a Negro's. But they hardly saw each other.

"Is this someone you used to know, John?" Victor asked.

"Who, Mike? No, I don't know him. Just what Rose told me about him coming up. But he's all alone in there. You can't abandon a man if he's in danger of being trapped by a forest fire!"

"That's better than risking five lives," Victor said.

"We aren't going to *risk* five lives! Burns and Harley'll know some way of getting in there. We can go around. Didn't you hear Burns say Bear Creek was over there? Nobody needs to go that doesn't want to, anyway!" John flung at them.

Burns and Harley came back from the ledge.

Unless the Wind Turns

"Well?" John shouted.

"We can make it," Harley shouted back. "Unless the wind turns on us. Little tough climbing up through that old windfall to where the creek comes off, though. All of you going?"

It was curious how still it could be in the woods in the midst of a fire. The unholy crackling of pitch-covered branches, the booming of falling logs, the awful mounting roar of the fire in the tops of the trees fell away or stood outside the small circle of sudden quiet between them. The bright light on their faces showed nothing. They looked comically alike, all made up for the same villain's role, lines of ferocity drawn in with strokes of black soot. They differed only in stature and the sound of their voices.

"I should think there would be an advantage in sending fresh men, accustomed to fire fighting and the woods, in after him," Victor said. He didn't look at John. John amused him by his vehemence. He fitted the "American type" as he thought of it. "John isn't subtle," Serena had told him.

"They're all needed on the fire. We need to get right in there, or we'll be too late if the fire keeps going," Harley said. He turned aside to talk to Burns about the route.

Walt smoothed his lips between two blackened

fingers, unconsciously, as he did in the hospital, deciding on a procedure with a sick child. In spite of himself, he said, "You're sure we can make it?"

"Of course we can," John answered quickly, "if we get going. You and Victor can go back and take care of the girls."

Victor smiled. "You mean that you might end by having to help the two of us if we went with you."

"Let's stick together," Walt said quickly.

"All right, then, we'll all go. Harley says there's no great danger unless the wind turns suddenly," John said.

Victor glanced at Walt. "They'll go faster without us, Walt. I doubt if we'd be of any great help." He hesitated a moment; then he went on, speaking louder to make sure he was heard. He looked at John while he was talking.

"You know you can't live where I have and see half a dozen of your friends disappear mysteriously, knowing that they won't ever come back, without acquiring a little different view of life. You cannot help people by . . ." he hunted for the American expression, "by pushing your neck out. That is why I left Austria."

John's mouth twisted unpleasantly. Victor moved around to the other side of John and spoke so low that Walt could not hear, "Walt would be of no use in the woods; he is not so stalwart."

John smiled a mocking kind of smile. "So you better take him back."

Victor's face tightened. "You are childish," he began, but John had walked over to Burns.

"They're going on back; can't we get started?"

"Come, Walt, we really cannot do any good," Victor said.

"Hell, no, I'm not going back," Walt said firmly. He slipped his canteen over his shoulder. "Let's go. On to Mike!" His teeth gleamed through the soot in a grin.

Burns turned to Victor. "Better tell the women not to expect any of us back before morning. It'll take quite a while. Tell Rose—" he glanced abstractedly across at the fire—"tell her not to worry about Mike. We'll get him out."

"All right." Victor smiled. Walt didn't look at him. John met his eyes an instant, then looked away.

"Good fortune!" Victor called, but he doubted whether they heard him.

He watched them disappear into the woods that were still unburned, but made red by the reflection of the wall of flame across the gulch. The four men were pigmy creatures beside the red lighted trees, helpless looking as they grew smaller. It was the small, helpless look of them that made him think of those colleagues of his, doctors at the Allgemeine Krankenhaus, but Jews. He had stood in his office and watched them going down the avenue after their dismissal. They had looked small and helpless. He had not been surprised when two of them committed suicide. A third was sent to a concentration camp, and a fourth disappeared; men he respected, valuable to science, useful to the university. No, he could not be worked up over an unknown youth by the name of Mike who might or might not be trapped in the woods. It was too bad that Walt felt he had to go.

As he started down through the old burn, he met some of the fire fighters.

"Hi!" one of them said, a boy in a kind of uniform. Victor nodded to him in return, smiling at the greeting.

"Looks like the fire's moving about twenty miles an hour," one boy yelled.

"Looks like it," he shouted back. He thought they looked at him curiously, wondering why he wasn't staying to fight fire with them; why he wasn't at it, singlehanded if need be.

"Well, boys," he could say to them, "I know when a thing is too big to fight. That's why I got out of Austria." The fire over there was low down then.

It hadn't . . . what was the expression John used? Oh, yes, crowned. The fire in Europe hadn't crowned then. But it had since. It was in the trees now, all right, moving with a roar and the same suffocating heat and smoke, seventy miles an hour—seventy at the least.

To get out had been the only wise thing to do. His opinions were clearly known. When the Jewish doctors were forced to resign, he had resigned in protest to decency. He wouldn't work with the new men they brought in, nor under rules that made scientific honesty impossible. After the invasion, it was not safe for him. So he had fled.

He hadn't gone back into danger's way after . . . to see whether Kathie was trapped. Walt would have, and that insufferable husband of Serena's, and they would have been uselessly destroyed for their foolhardiness.

But it bothered him that he hadn't heard from Kathie or from Paul. He'd left money with Paul for her, and he'd sent some since, but he didn't know whether she had ever received it. Lizzie looked like Kathie, but she lacked Kathie's independence, her fire. Fire, always back to fire! Serena looked nothing like Kathie, but she had her way of standing apart.

A burning brand blew past his face. He watched

where it landed and ran at it to put it out, but it did not stop his train of thought.

Kathie wasn't a Jewess, but she had been outspoken. It was known that she had helped Jews to escape. It was not safe for her to stay in Vienna. Did she hate him for leaving? Surely, she could have found some way to get word to him so that he would know that she was safe.

The smoke came at him like a cloud of poison gas, choking him, burning his eyes. Then a fresh wave of heat seared his face and arms, like a blast from a flame-thrower. He thought he heard someone yell and stopped to listen. Then he saw another of the uniformed boys on his way up. He waved to him.

No, it was only sense. If the fire was too big to fight, you got out of its way. He covered his eyes against another wave of smoke. A low cedar burned with a staccato rattling like the stutter of a machine gun hidden in the bushes.

The wind had turned! The fire had been a mile from here when they came over this ground an hour ago. He was almost surrounded by it. He broke into a run.

Harley went first, then Burns, then Walt, then John. John was impatient of the slow pace they set.

Going through the old blowdown was hard, but he was indifferent to the difficulties of climbing over logs, having his leg caught between two logs, stopping to extricate himself, of the snarl of stuff that scratched at his face and tore at his hair. Sweat poured from him. The heat was so great it felt as though the whole old heap of logs would burst into flame again. The roar was not so loud, because they were sheltered from the fire across the gulch. It made him think of the roar the hot wind made against his ears when he drove eighty to ninety miles an hour in an open car across Montana. This had the same unreality. In the car, he drove so fast the gray road and the sky and open empty prairie made a tunnel. Only there was no purpose in driving so fast. You beat your last record out here by two hours, but you always had to stop finally and get out of the car with the empty roar of the wind still in your ears. This was different. He had a purpose. They were driving through to rescue Rose's Mike for her.

The smoke was worse now. It got in his eyes again and stuck in his throat. Walt stumbled over a log, and he stopped to help him up. Smoke bothered him, too.

"Gosh, did you ever feel such heat!" he yelled to Walt.

The crazy beaver pile of dead logs was endless. If the fire across the gulch didn't light the whole forest up like a jack o'lantern, you couldn't go an inch. When the smoke cleared, you could see the flames again. They looked higher; seventy-five, fifty feet anyway. Queer how you could be so near and yet safe from it. It was spreading. The whole west fork must be on fire.

It was like the war. That was Europe over there. He was in America, trying to help without getting over there; watching for spot fires. If the wind should change though, you couldn't keep it from spreading. The fire could leap the gulch like nobody's business. This side would be on fire. The windfall stuff and the standing timber beyond it were so dry there wasn't even a wet hiss when a spot fire struck. It was waiting to catch fire, like America.

He must tell Serena that. She would say, "Why, John, how bright of you." He'd tell her, too, that her everlasting Victor was a brand sailing across from the fire. Not wanting to do his part when he got here, trying to excuse his not going by saying Walt would be no good in the woods. John saw a brand light and catch fire. He ran for it across the blowdown, walking the fallen timbers like a bridge. He beat at the new blaze with the rage his mind felt for Victor.

Unless the Wind Turns

The spot fires were coming faster. Brands carried farther in. In an instant, it seemed, they were all trying to stop new blazes. Fires sprang up behind them. It was getting bad in here. The air was full of sparks and the quick, fierce crackle. A limb of a snag fell not more than a yard in front of him.

"It's coming this way!" Walt yelled, and his face was stretched with fear. John saw his face. It was like the time when they were boys at camp and Walt tried to swim the lake. He couldn't make it, and they had to haul him into the boat.

"We'll make it!" John yelled to him, trying to wait for him; but you couldn't wait. He went back to try to stay behind him. He was caught up in something that took all the energy and brain he had. Wasn't this what he had always wanted? This was something to fight. He felt he could hack his way through if he had to go straight through the center of the fire. The smoke and heat tore at his throat, but the ache was part of him.

"All right?" he yelled to Walt, who was bent over double, coughing. "We're coming!" he yelled to Burns, working up ahead of him. Where was Harley going? He saw the ranger plunging away to the right, holding his arm up to protect his head from flying brands. He saw Burns pointing.

Then he saw: the fire was closing in on them from

the left. He looked away quickly. He began to run. He had to watch the ground to find a place to step in the windfall. In spite of himself and the urgent need to hurry, he saw how the red light lit up caves in between the logs. At a glance he could see more than he'd ever seen: moss yellow-green in the glare, a toadstool growing out of it, red-edged, the blades of grass and a withered stalk of Indian paintbrush. The bark of the logs was different, one smooth— that must be poplar—and the other rough. It was like looking into one of those glass Easter eggs when you were a kid and seeing a whole magic world inside.

The fire was closer, but for this moment he wasn't afraid, he thought with a queer elation. This was the way men must feel in the war. A bomber lost above a hostile country, knowing he wouldn't get back, not caring. It wasn't bravery, it was just a state of mind you got into. He'd always wondered how men could do some of the things they did, wondered if he could. It was a free feeling, free from yourself and your own life. If he ever got out of the fire alive, he'd sit down and think about this. . . .

The smoke wrapped around him, filling the aperture between the dead snags standing in the windfall. He walked into a snag.

"Watch out!" he yelled to Walt, looking around

to try to see him. There was no answering call. The smoke shut him in with his own voice. A tree crashed near him. He went ahead, holding his arms before him to ward off falling limbs as Harley had done. Then the smoke lifted and he faced live flame. There must be green timber in here to burn like that. He must have crossed the windfall. He turned and ran. He fell over a log and picked himself up and ran again. He didn't dare look behind him. Where were the others? He tried to yell again, but his voice was too hoarse and dry. The roar was too loud. Where was he? A minute ago they were all together. Now he was alone.

The bravery he had felt before was gone. Panic rose in him. Run as long as he could before the fire closed him in. Run . . . keep running . . . he was babbling like an idiot.

He kept falling, and swore as he picked himself up. Anyway he would be burned to death trying to save Rose's Mike. . . . "Why, you damned liar!" he swore back at himself, "You got yourself into this. It was exciting, and you thought you were a pretty good woodsman and a hero."

It was so hot he couldn't stand it. He stumbled and fell and lay there. Let the fire come, he couldn't get any farther. With a sound close to a sob he buried his face in the earth, digging into it with his nails. He got his canteen and drank, pouring the last drops over his face. He noticed the canvas covering of the canteen and saw how it was scorched. Over the bulge of the canteen he stared at the fire moving inexorably toward him.

For the moment now he could breathe; the pain in his chest eased. His mind cleared. He must work his way downslope to reach the creek . . . unless the creek were dry! There was a bank . . . he remembered from long ago.

If he could reach the creek . . . he didn't dare stand up; if he could crawl! He dug in with his heels and pushed, half crawling, half lunging ahead. There was a half-burned log lying on the ground . . . he shoved ahead, inch by inch, until he lay alongside it, on the lee side. . . . That was what Burns said, "Keep your face down . . . breathe near the earth . . . don't lose your head . . . a man can stand more than he thinks. . . ."

His jacket was smoking. He beat at it frantically with his fist, rolling over to smother the smoldering edge. His panic rose . . . he was going to burn to death. . . .

He lay closer to the log, digging in the hot ground with his hands, burying his face against the dirt.

He could breathe a little easier . . . the fire roared in the trees just back of him. He heard the limbs of trees crashing down to the ground. Here there was a break in the timber but the fire-heated breath of the wind was unbearable . . . he closed his eyes. He couldn't last long like this.

"We've got to work over to the right. I'll go ahead. You hold on to me," Burns shouted in Walt's ear. "Where's John?"

"Don't know," Walt shouted back, struggling for breath. The smoke was so thick they couldn't see four feet ahead. Trees crashed near them. They heard the boom, wondering if the next tree would hit them. Walt closed his eyes and hung on to Burns.

Even with the woods on fire Burns seemed to know his way. They came straight across to the shallow creek. It barely trickled over the stones, but there was no sound of water in the roar. Burns motioned Walt to lie full length in the shallow bed. Steam went up from their clothes. They covered their faces with water. The water that came down from glacial snow high in the mountains was warm and black with cinders. Something touched Walt's hand. He picked it up, and it was a dead fish, floating, white belly up. They drank and couldn't get enough, and it didn't help the ache in their throats.

"Harley's gone to find an old mine entrance,"

Tuesday

Burns shouted. "We can't stay here." He cupped his hands and yelled for John. He shook his head. "He's gotten separated. He knows these woods." But the look in his face was not comforting.

Walt nodded dumbly. Once it seemed to him that he saw clear blue flame spring up in the air like a will-o'-the-wisp, and he dug deeper into the stream bed and covered his face with water, sobbing into the creek, knowing no one could hear him.

Harley appeared out of the woods, looking unreal, with his hair singed off across the front and his eyebrows burned clean. They soaked whatever they could in the stream. Walt emptied his emergency rations and covered his head with the wet sack. Burns soaked his hat.

"When we get to the mine it'll be all right," Walt told himself in his pain. He stared ahead into the burning woods and tried to see the cool inside of a mine. He had been down in an anthracite mine in Pennsylvania once. Water trickled over the side, he remembered. It was damp and clammy cool.

The smoke strangled him. Pain pressed its thumb on each eyeball, trying to push it out of its socket. He couldn't get his breath. He couldn't stand it. . . . "Oh, my God!" he groaned, but the words were articulate only in his mind.

✦

"He's all right. The smoke got him," Walt heard Harley saying. He opened his eyes.

"It got you for a moment. You passed out. We dragged you in here. Have a swallow. Harley found the mine shaft. It's kind of hot, but it's better than burning to death out there," Burns said, holding the canteen to Walt's mouth.

Walt looked around. The place was insufferable. Timbers at the mouth of it were on fire. Burns and Harley were dashing wet things against them. He had to close his eyes against the smoke that rushed into the cave. He couldn't stand it, couldn't breathe; better to get out and run for it.

"John, I can't breathe." Walt tried to get to his knees. Burns forced him back on the ground.

"Yes, you can. Lie on the ground; more air . . ." Burns' words came in gasps. He was having trouble, himself.

"John! Listen to me, John!" Walt cried out, but no one answered. He had to bury his face again against the dirt.

Harley and Burns lay on the ground. The roar of the fire was loud in the cave, but the agonized breathing of the three men was louder. They couldn't see for the smoke. Something dropped on Walt's head. Half groggy, he reached around to feel it. His hand recoiled from a furry body. It was a dead squirrel. He threw it weakly toward the opening. It landed just outside the entrance and a sudden flare sprang up in the cloud of smoke.

They'd all die in here, like the squirrel. He fought to get up. He tried to figure shrewdly how he could get past Burns. He tried crawling.

"Here!" Harley had found a trickle of water in the mine. He put something wet over Walt's face. For a minute the acidlike smoke cutting into his lungs eased.

A tree fell across the front of the mine shaft. The smoke thickened. Someone groaned. Had he groaned? Walt bit his lips and pressed his face closer against the earth. He groaned again.

Burns wet his felt hat; the trickle of water was so small it took forever. He pressed it over his face, cutting out the smoke for an instant. He let out his breath in an agonized sigh. "I should have known better . . . let those two come with us, Harley," he muttered. His lungs felt like they did when he was gassed in France. They'd given him whiskey then. He could do with some right now. No, water would be better . . . drinking too much lately. The boy had looked at him kind of queer the other day, as though he guesed it.

Smoke crowded into the mine shaft, wave after wave, pushing out the air. There was no thinking, only fighting for breath. The three men groveled on the dirt, struggling to live. Harley crawled to the opening again. Smoke and flames rushed at him. No man could live five minutes outside the cave. If they could last, somehow, till morning! . . . Walt tried to crawl past his legs. With all the strength he had, Harley kicked him back into the cave.

"We can't live in here, Burns!" Walt screamed out.

"You can't live outside," Harley answered in a voice that was more groan than words.

Walt clawed at the rock for the trickle of water. He closed his eyes against the pain of his eyeballs.

Burns fell over him when he tried to get to the water. He wet the bandanna that was over his mouth, but he was too weak to move any farther. Walt's groans had stopped.

Harley lay against the opening of the mine shaft, his face against the earth, struggling for breath. He'd been badly burned when he dashed away to hunt for the mine. His burns ached. He gritted his teeth against the dirt.

WEDNESDAY

10

"ROSE, lie down again, please!" Serena begged. Rose made no answer, and walked away from the fire out into the open meadow. The wild light of the fire that seemed to stand just above the rim of the hill showed her arms wrapped around herself and her head leaning painfully toward one shoulder. Then her head straightened and she walked again.

"She's walking her pains like an aborigine; she'd be better off if she'd lie still," Lizzie murmured.

"She is in labor; I'm sure, Lizzie," Serena said almost fearfully. "I wish we knew what we should do. Why don't we, Lizzie?"

"Well, I don't know why we should. I've never seen a woman have a child. I had twilight sleep when I had Buster; it was a blank to me."

"But we should know what to do. Women used to. My grandmother was an expert. We act like morons," Serena railed.

"They said at the fire camp that they'd get word to Walt or Victor as fast as they could."

"I'm going to make her come back and lie down," Serena said, going to her.

She put her arm around Rose's shoulders awkwardly. Serena was not demonstrative. But Rose's shoulders held rigid.

"The fire's getting nearer Bear Creek all the time," she whispered as though to herself. Serena pressed her arm tighter around Rose. She had never in her life tried to comfort anyone.

"How do you feel?" she asked timidly.

'The pains are bad, and they come regular. I don't care though; I don't want the kid if Mike don't get out alive."

"But he's going to get out all right. What about the others? They're up in there. I don't know whether John's safe or not." As she said it, she realized that she hadn't worried about him at all. "Come on back and lie down, Rose."

"I can't," Rose said, but she let herself be led back to the fire. Lizzie made her a hot toddy, looking like a witch bending over the kettle on the fire, her hair loose on her shoulders, her face furrowed with worry and sleeplessness.

"What time is it?" Lizzie whispered after Rose had lain still for some time.

Wednesday

Serena held her arm to the firelight. "About four. Here comes someone." Silently they watched.

"Why, it's Vic again," Serena exclaimed. "I'll go meet him." She ran across the hot, firelit meadow. "Victor!" she called softly, her voice light with relief. She ran to him and caught hold of his arm.

"Oh, Vic, Rose is in labor, we think. She's having terrible pains. We don't know what to do for her. Oh, Vic, I'm so glad you're here." She was clinging to him.

"Maybe she just imagines it," Victor said. He was still panting. "John and the others have gone to rescue Mike. I'm the official messenger to the ladies. They won't be back . . ." before morning, he had been about to say, but he changed it quickly, "before afternoon." It had taken him all night to find his way back.

"Are they safe?" Serena asked quickly.

"Oh, yes, they're all right," he said lightly. "Burns and the ranger are with them. I couldn't see that I would be of very much assistance, so I came back. Your husband seemed to think I was frightened."

"How silly!" Serena said mechanically, but she could see John. It was queer for Victor to turn back if the rest went on, but she thrust the thought out of her mind. Then she realized how fast he was breathing, and saw the torn, burned state of his clothes and that his face was burned in two places.

"Are you all right? Your face is burned."

"Just a little singed coming through the fire. I think the wind changed. The fire's crossed the gulch. Everything beyond the reef is on fire. We may have to get out of here, too."

"Victor, do you think . . . what about Mike?" Her own voice was a whisper.

"I fear for him. I think the others will have to turn around and come back before they reach him."

Serena caught her breath. They both watched the flames. The whole upper end of the canyon was on fire.

"Say, it's just possible that Rose and I might be interested in talking to Victor, too!" Lizzie called out.

"Don't tell Rose," Serena whispered quickly. "And, Vic, if she really is in labor, I think we ought to get her some place in town."

"She's all right here as far as that goes." Before he had a chance to get his breath, Serena was worrying him about this girl, he thought irritably.

"Not just out in the mountains like this," Serena objected. "I thought we could get her back to town in one of the forest service trucks. There ought to be some kind of a hospital there."

"That's quite a distance on a rough road."

"I know, but if we started right away . . ." They were walking back toward the campfire.

"Plenty of women have had babies in fields before now."

Lizzie came to meet them. "Really, you're driving Rose frantic, stopping to talk out here!"

"It looks like an army camp down there," Victor remarked, unhurried.

"Men have been coming in all night. We've watched them. There must be hundreds in there," Lizzie said.

"They need them," Victor said grimly. "Even so, I don't think there's much they can do, the wind's so bad. The fire seems to whip it up."

"How will they get it stopped then?" Serena asked.

"Oh, I suppose it'll burn itself out up against the rocks at the top. There's snow up there and no timber. The fire against those glacial drifts must be quite a sight. I would like a picture of that."

The girls hovered anxiously by while Victor knelt by Rose, asking her questions. He laid his hand on her as she lay there. Rose turned away from him.

"Lie still!" Victor said sharply. Serena bit her lip. Lizzie knelt down beside her, trying to hold Rose's tight clenched fist. Rose sat up suddenly, her face pinched and white in the firelight, her eyes blazing.

"Then tell me where Mike is? Why doesn't he come? What were you talking about out there?" Her voice rose to a scream.

"The others have gone for him," Victor said. "They'll bring him back with them. You aren't going to help him any by getting yourself into such a state. Lie quietly now. Obey, please."

For a few minutes she lay still under his hands; then she burst into sobs and rolled over, hiding her face in the sleeping bag. The legs of her jeans had climbed up to her knees, and the firelight showed her bare legs and the holes in the heels of her socks.

Victor came over to the fire where Serena was frying eggs and bacon. Lizzie stayed with Rose. The coffee boiled up, and Serena grabbed the pot quickly to move it back from the heat.

"She's . . . do you think she is?"

"Oh, yes, she's having regular contractions, all right."

"Do you . . . can you deliver a baby, Vic?" Serena asked.

Victor laughed. "Well, I haven't attended any woman since I was a student. The peasant women never have doctors and, of course, there are more midwives there than here. I've paid more than one woman to let me take her into the dispensary.

Once we sterilized a woman with ten children, and the nurse told her about it. When I went to see how she was doing, she took my hand; I thought she was going to kiss it, but instead, she bit me." He laughed. "I've still got the marks of her teeth in my hand here." He held it over for Serena to see.

Serena turned the bacon in the frying pan without speaking. For some perverse reason, she would not be amused.

"I'll go and see if I can get some of this grime off," Victor said. "Is there some soap around?" For a man who had narrowly escaped death this was a casual reception, he thought wryly.

Serena went over to Rose. "Rose, John and Burns and Walt have gone to help Mike. Don't worry. They're all together. The ranger's with them. And there are hundreds of men on the fire now. There's nothing to worry about."

Rose still kept her face buried. Her shoulders moved convulsively. Serena and Lizzie looked helplessly at each other.

"Listen, Rose," Serena began again. "Do you think you could stand to ride in the truck? We'll go back to town so we can take care of you decently."

"I'm all right here. I don't care where I am," Rose answered. Then the pain made her writhe away from them again.

"This is no place, Rose. There are all those men camped over there, and it'll be roasting hot here when the sun comes up. Mike would want you in a better place."

Rose sat up, wiping her face on her sleeve. "Sure, I can ride," she said like a child that means to be obedient now.

Lizzie and Serena and Victor ate their breakfast in the queer, uncertain light of morning that came dimly through the pall of smoke. While they were eating, a plane came over, sweeping low over the fire camp and rising again to go over the reef.

"It's six-thirty," Lizzie said. "Shouldn't they be coming by now?"

"It takes almost three hours to get back over that trail. I don't suppose there is any trail by now, either," Victor said.

Serena looked at him drinking his coffee, wondering how he could be here when the others were on the fire. It was lucky that he was here so he could take care of Rose, but how could he leave the other men?

"How far up the trail were you when they got word to you about Rose?" Serena asked abruptly.

"Oh, I was nearly back here. One of the last crew brought word."

"I don't see why Walt didn't come with you if there are plenty of men in there," Lizzie worried.

Victor smiled at them. "Then why did I come out? That bothers you."

Both girls were abashed. Serena busied herself with the coffee. Lizzie was watching the fire.

"Because I couldn't see the point of inexperienced men like Walt and myself, even John, going in on that trip. You Americans rush out after danger rather eagerly, you know. I think this Mike, unless he got out of the woods before they started after him, was very likely burned to death."

Lizzie caught her breath. "Oh, no, Victor, that couldn't be. Rose couldn't stand it."

Victor lighted his cigarette. "You see what I mean? You're used to reading about horror and death and war, not to facing it. That makes a difference. I simply state the probable facts, and you think me heartless. . . ."

He went on talking about realistic European psychology, but Serena had begun picking up the dishes. She poured out the coffee that was left, instead of drinking the last cup as she usually did.

"I think we ought to get moving," she murmured. Back home Victor's leisurely way of talking, of growing interested in his subject and running on about it, excited her. At this moment, it seemed shallow and heartless. She was impatient to be on their way. All the time she was conscious of Rose.

"I'll go over to the fire camp and get a truck," Victor said.

"Look at the sun," Lizzie said. "It looks like a poached egg." The sun was so hidden under the smoke you could look at it without squinting. The uncertain reddish light had changed to white, but the sky was swollen and black along the edges, like an infected area of skin. The air smelled of smoke. There was a curious emptiness. No camp robber or chickadee uttered a sound. No live thing stirred except a grasshopper, springing out of the grass with a noise as loud as a shot, and flies buzzing aimlessly over the bacon grease in the frying pan.

"Do you suppose we'd hear anything about the fire over the radio?" Lizzie asked. She had lost her interest in the war news.

Serena glanced warningly at Rose.

"I'll turn it low," Lizzie said.

They bent over it, screened from Rose's view by a sprawling Juniper. A song by some hill-billy trio jangled against their ears. Lizzie moved the knob.

"There," Serena whispered.

". . . owing to extreme burning conditions, it may not be humanly possible to control the fire to-day. The wind, throughout last night, was of ex-

166

tremely high velocity. This wind is continuing, and the forecast for today indicates that wind will increase in velocity throughout the day. Alarm is felt concerning the safety of Mike Logan, twenty, logging north of Bear Creek. A party, headed by ranger Harley, has gone in for him. Further news of this fire will be broadcast. . . ." Lizzie snapped off the dial.

"Was that the radio?" Rose called.

"Just some hill-billy music and an advertisement," Lizzie answered, going to her.

Victor came back in one of the forest service trucks with some CCC boys to help push the truck out of the stream. They laid a sleeping bag on the floor of the truck.

"I can sit up," Rose said sulkily, climbing in to sit on the wooden bench along the side.

Lizzie stayed behind with the camp stuff, to wait for the men when they came back from the fire.

"I certainly am the little homebody," Lizzie said. "Or would you call me the sweetheart of the fire camp?" But she drew Victor aside. "You do think they'll come soon, Vic? This isn't my idea of fun, you know, waiting here alone."

"I wouldn't count on their showing up before noon," Victor said.

"All right, Rose?" Serena asked from time to

time, as the truck bumped and rocked over the logging road.

"Yup," Rose answered. She seemed better moving than lying in a heap on the sleeping bag.

Victor whistled, and they were startled when Rose joined in.

"Mike 'n' me used to play that for dances last year, but folks don't like waltzes so much any more," she told them, and then was silent so long Victor glanced back at her. She was crying.

"Gosh, this is the worst stomick ache I ever had."

"Take another aspirin," Serena urged.

Rose took it. "Aspirin don't seem to do no good," she complained, half apologetically.

Serena felt as though every leaf hanging listlessly in the hot, dull light were impressed on her brain. They crossed the meadow where they had hunted grouse, but no one spoke of it. The trucks last night had left deep tracks across the meadow. The heavy choking smell of smoke was here, too; and wherever the trees opened out to show a wider space of sky, they could see the reddish tinge.

She studied Victor as he sat across from her in the truck. She remembered the day she had heard about his resigning his professorship because of the dismissal of his colleagues; how he had given up his position and his home in Vienna for an ideal, really, because he wouldn't live or work under the Nazis. She had admired him for his courage.

Later on, when she knew him better, she had tried to tell him how she admired his action. He had made light of it. She remembered what he had said, sitting out on the bench by the tennis court.

"I have no brief for the Jews, understand, but I'd defend them against anyone who tried to prevent them from teaching. If you submit to the restriction of intellectual freedom, you are lost. A man is a pitiable thing if he isn't willing to sacrifice something for what he believes is important. Walt or your husband would have done the same thing." She remembered guiltily that she had wondered whether easygoing John would or not.

It was queer that Victor had been on his way back when the message about Rose reached him, that he had wanted to get back to safety. . . . She frowned a little as she sat looking out the end of the truck.

They didn't try to talk. Victor and Rose and Serena sat bracing themselves against the jolts. The heat beat down on the canvas-covered top of the truck. Out the end they could see the smoke clouds that drifted lower over the woods.

Suddenly, Serena heard Rose catch her breath with a little cry which penetrated strangely above the heavy roar of the truck. She saw Victor slide across to her side and saw him nod. She couldn't hear what Victor said to Rose, but she could see Rose's misery-filled eyes.

Victor slid along the bench to where Serena was sitting.

"The waters broke. I don't believe we better try to make it into town, or we'll be having the birth right here in the truck. I'll have them let us out here."

Serena looked out at the lodgepole pines climbing up the sloping ground. The shade was thin, and a dry heat rose from the ground.

"What about that cabin of John's, Vic? We must be somewhere near it. Can't the men carry her over there?"

They stopped the truck, but Rose insisted on walking.

"I know where the cabin is," Rose said. "It can't be more than a quarter of a mile from here, because the trail an' the logging road both follow the creek."

Victor nodded. "In a few hours we shall want one of you to stop for us to take us on into town," he told the CCC boy. "I shall tie a white handkerchief to this branch when we have need of you. The driver who sees it is to stop and walk in for us; I shall mark the way."

"Prob'ly Mr. Jackson could get an ambulance out

for you," the boy said with a marked East Side accent.

"I don't want any ambulance," Rose muttered.

"Very well, the truck then," Victor agreed.

"Yes, sir," the boy said, letting in his clutch; but before the truck roared off, Serena heard him say, "Hell, does that guy think I'm a taxi driver?" and his companion's reply, "Naw, he just wants to play drop the handkerchief with you."

They made their way, a curious procession: Rose stopping frequently to rest, and then going doggedly on through the woods.

"How are you?" Victor asked once.

"The pain's so bad I could bust," Rose answered.

But soon they hit the trail that they had come over on horseback; Victor went ahead to open the cabin.

"You'll have to break into it, Vic!" Serena called after him. "John locked it."

"Well, that wouldn't stop me!" Victor answered, smiling.

11

SERENA had never been more grateful to see any-thing than she was to see the tar-paper roof of John's cabin. She wondered if this was the way women felt after they'd lived in trailers, moving from place to place, camping out while their husbands did what-ever they could find to do. There was something in a woman that made her want a house to live in, to have her baby born in anyway.

Victor had untied the mattresses from the rafters and made up a bed on one of the bunks. The cabin was hot and close, but the half-dark was a relief. Serena helped Rose out of her clothes into a worn pajama top. She had never been around sick peo-ple nor helped anyone. She did it awkwardly, with a little embarrassment.

"It must be good to get into bed, isn't it?"

"Yeah." Tears rolled out of Rose's eyes, and she hid her face in an old school pillow of John's. Serena stood helplessly beside her.

Wednesday

"Don't cry, Rose; it might make your pains worse." But Rose didn't seem to hear her.

Victor was sitting on the step of the cabin. She sat down beside him. Yesterday, from here, they could see the snow-capped peak of some mountain. Now it was completely lost in the sullen murky air that shut them into a smaller world. She looked at her watch. It was only eight-thirty.

"Why don't you go in on that other bunk and get a little sleep?" Victor suggested.

"I couldn't sleep. Can't we do something for her, Vic?"

"There's nothing to do. She's a healthy young animal. I brought along a little scrub brush that Burns had, to scrub with, and some green soap and gauze from the emergency kit. We'll boil the brush after a bit and have some boiled water ready."

"I'll do that now," Serena said, eagerly seizing upon it. Inside the dark little cabin, she rummaged around in the lean-to kitchen. John had labeled the cans, and his printing that always tipped backward looked familiar. She started a fire with the kindling and paper she found by the stove, wondering how long ago John had left it there.

"Leave her alone for a while. She won't fuss so much if you're not right with her," Victor said from the porch.

Serena sat on the porch listening to Rose turn and moan. "I wish we could find out that Mike was all right. She wouldn't mind this so much then."

Victor shrugged. He had been silent so long she glanced at him, feeling his strangeness.

"But what takes them so long, Victor?"

"You should see the woods. I think they had to turn back."

"Can't you go in and say something to her, Vic? Something comforting, you know."

Victor went inside. Serena hovered by the door. She heard Victor's few questions; his words, "You ought to get rid of it pretty soon, now, then you'll feel all right. Stop crying and get a little sleep."

He was kind enough, but there was something automatic and impersonal about his kindness. Serena went in and made some tea, but Rose took a few swallows and turned away. When she whispered something, Serena had to lean close to hear her.

"Mike'll think I'm pretty poor not to hang on to the baby."

"Of course he won't, Rose. He'll just be glad you're all right." But nothing she said seemed to help. Rose held her hand, so she sat beside her, looking around the small room.

This was the place John used to talk so much about. It was no more than a shack, really. Her eyes traveled from object to object: John's fishing rod, the butterfly net; he must have been a queer boy to like coming up here alone and living. He even used to cook for himself.

Serena wasn't used to sitting idle. She moved her hand tentatively, but Rose's fingers tightened. Victor was so quiet on the porch he must have gone to sleep. She felt the stillness filling the cabin. It was nearly nine in the morning, but you couldn't tell it from the light. It might have been seven o'clock at night, the cabin was so dark.

How funny that John had come way back here just before they were married!

"I didn't do much that time but think what it was going to be like having you," he had said.

What had he expected? That she would be more absorbed in him . . . more passionate, maybe. Even to herself she avoided the word. She couldn't pretend to be something she wasn't. And John meant more than that, anyway. "Our marriage just doesn't mean enough to either of us," John had said. What more could it mean?

Rose moved restlessly, pulling her knees up under her chin and thrusting them down again. Serena could see the perspiration on her face. She wondered shyly if Rose loved her Mike passionately. Then Rose turned over toward her, and Serena drew away her hand that was cramped from lying across the bed so long.

"I knew it would hurt, but not like this. When I used to get scared about how it would be, Mike always promised he'd be right by me. Mike's helped lots of mares with their colts. I wouldn't mind if he was here."

Serena gave her two more aspirin and a drink of water, to be doing something for her. She thought of Lizzie saying, "When I had Buster, I had twilight sleep." She would have, too, when she came to have a child, and go to the hospital, and it would all be easy. Things were muffled for them; the sharp edge of pain was blunted; that was right, but maybe the edge of feeling other things was, too. But how could you help that? Your life was the way it was. Hers and Lizzie's and the lives of the women she knew were pretty much the same. They were a lot alike, and so were their husbands; one was wittier than another, one played better golf or bridge or made more money or drank more. They all seemed a little futile, in a way. Victor had seemed different. Beside him, John was dull. John had nothing to offer except stories about his boyhood, about the men who worked for him, or his Aero Engines. But today, it was Victor who seemed insensitive; almost lacking.

If Walt were here, she was sure he would be more

of a comfort to Rose. After all, that was what doctors were for.

Rose lay quietly again, and Serena moved softly around the room. She looked at John's books on the shelf, reading the titles: *Stalky & Co., Greenhough's Latin Grammar;* that came from the summer he flunked Latin and he'd wanted to stay in Princeton at the tutoring school. His father had been disgusted, and told him to take his grammar to the mountains and learn it himself. And he had. He'd told her that once; he was proud of being able to do it. In the beginning, John used to tell her all kinds of things about when he was a boy, and about his father and Burns. She had listened politely, not too much interested; they seemed such little things. Now they came back to her.

She opened an old composition book. Only a few pages were written on. John wouldn't mind her reading it; he'd be pleased that she was interested. The first entry was written in pencil. A stub of a pencil was still tied to the book by a dirty string. The writing was crooked and round, yet somehow like John's.

At my cabin.   *July 12, 1922*

I am going to keep a diary of every single thing that happens at Burns' this summer so I can read it next winter in school. I wish I could stay here all year round.

Unless the Wind Turns

I asked Dad, but he promised Mother he'd send me back east to school. When you promise something to somebody who dies, it becomes sakred. Mother didn't like Montana. The wind made her nervus and no trees. I like the wind and don't mind no trees. There are so many trees at school they make it gluemy. Today I saddled and rode Flash all alone. I helped Burns get the horses in. It is 8 o'clock and I am going to hit the hay . . . that is what Burns says.

August 2

I haven't wrote as much as I sed I would, but I am too sleepy at nite and busy other times. Somthing swell has happined. Burns says I can have this cabin for my own if I pay for the lease, which is 16 BUCKS a year. I can because I get 1 Buck a week and have got $6.71 on hand. Dad will give me my allowance ahead. I have come up here to spend the nite ALONE. I have my gun and flashlight but only 2 bullits; Burns says 2 is enough to get your man.

August 3

Morning. I slept all night ALONE, with the door wide open. There were lots of noises, but I wasn't afraid (except a little at first). There was a pack rat on the roof. I didn't shoot him, but will next time. I got my own breakfast. It was swell.

August 10

Burns is mad at me, and Slim who works for Burns says I'm just a dude after all and don't have enough sense to be a real Westerner. It is because I was sitting on the steps of Burnses cabin reading the funnies when a stalliun from Rankin's ranch came over the hill. The sorrel mare got xcited and winnied and stuck her ears up. The stalliun actally stood up on his hind legs against the coral, and so did the mare. Then the mare jumped the fence like a circus horse. Burns says I shuld have driven off the stalliun because I new the sorrel mare was going to be bred to Kingses, instead of sitting there and watching them go. It was bad because it takes so long to make a colt, longer than a baby even. Maybe the sorrel mare liked the work horse better and is sekretly glad. If I was a mare I would want to go with the stalliun I liked best.

Serena smiled to herself above the diary. That was like John. Then she remembered what John had said that night after she asked Victor to come on the trip. "Of course, if you like him, take him along; that's the thing to do."

There was a big gap between entries. The next was November, 1930. John was eighteen then. The writing was in ink and slanted more firmly to the right.

Got into Piegan City yesterday morning and drove right out to Burns' place. Dad came with me. We came on up to the cabin and spent the night. I think Burns would have liked to come, too, but Dad seemed to want to come off alone with me. Plenty cold. It started snowing in the night. Dad woke me up to tell me. We got to talking, and he said he wished he'd come up here with me more when I was growing up, and that he hadn't kept so close to the mill. He told me he'd put a lot of money into Will Cannon's oil well up on the Highline, half because it looked like a sure thing and half because of Cannon. He and Dad were out here together in the early days. The well didn't come in, and they lost everything they put into it. Dad still has the mill, but I guess he feels pretty poor. He acted almost guilty telling me about it. He said there was enough for me to finish school, but nothing except a job in the mill when I was through. I told him that was all right by me. I guess I don't get to Europe in June!

Got up at four and had breakfast ready when Dad woke up. He looks old when he's asleep. I never thought of him as being old before, but after all, he's really fifty-six.

Great walking up the trail half way to Bear Creek. The snow was a foot deep. Saw tracks everywhere. Saw a 7pt. elk, pretty as you please, coming out of the timber. We both saw him at the same time, but Dad said for me to go ahead. I got him, first shot. He is a beauty. Sure glad Dad let me come back here for the hunting season. He didn't tell the dean it was for hunting when he wrote for me to come, though!

Dad wanted to go on up toward the divide to see if he could get a mountain goat. Dad said he liked those fellows better than anything else in the mountains. He said that not many animals can stand it way up there alone, but that the goats get down to bare rock and manage to live. "That's what I like about Burns," Dad said. Dad's never talked to me so much before.

We saw a mountain sheep but no goat. Came back

here and had a hot toddy Dad made. He's death on me drinking, so I was surprised. All he said was, "You want to lay off the bathtub gin and bootleg liquor or you'll spoil your taste for the real thing."

Dad's asleep now. We're going back to town in the morning, and I'll take the seven o'clock train East. I guess Dad gets awfully lonesome here in winter. I tried to tell him he ought to come to New York this winter and come out to school. I said, "Doesn't it get pretty lonesome for you?" He said, "I feel like a mountain goat sometimes." I never knew he was like this.

There was only one more entry in March, 1935.

Dad died last week suddenly at the office in the mill. Nobody was with him. He was staying after time. The night watchman found him. He hadn't written for two or three weeks. Last time was just a sentence saying, "Remember you can't spend all the money in the world even if you try. Take it easy." and the check. I guess he was really having hard going. He'd just agreed to sell out to a big chain of grain elevators. He wouldn't have done that if he could have helped it.

I came out here with Burns after the funeral. This morning there was a chinook, and now it's like spring. Everything is melting. That helps, somehow. I snow-shoed up here from Burns' place, but I'll be walking back. This is a lonely place in winter, all right.

I'm going back to town tomorrow to go through Dad's things. Mr. Angle at the mill said I could have a job with the company when I got through school if I wanted it. Dad had insisted on that. I told him I'd let him know. If it were still Dad's, it would be different. The opening with Aero Engines looks better to me for an engineer. Reading about our hunting trip makes me miss Dad more. That's the only time I ever really talked to him.

Serena had to take the composition book over to the window. She forgot about Rose and Victor. John had come out here in '36 before they were married, but he hadn't written anything. She was disappointed. She flipped over the empty pages. There was something written on the last page, without any date.

A place that you keep going back to in your life is always more than a place. It's a kind of measuring ground and a philosophy and a hide-out. It can hurt so much that you come away and never want to go back to it, but it's there in your mind all the same. Everybody should have one; perhaps everyone does, if it's only the corner drugstore or Grant's tomb, or where you went to school. This cabin's mine. When you get back to it, it makes you sort out things and leave some behind that you won't be needing. Then you take away with you what you really care about.

That didn't sound like John. She and John didn't talk about what they thought, or did he try to sometimes? They weren't alone very much, anyway. Lizzie and Walt or Matt . . . someone was usually over. Then she remembered that that was what

John had said that night after she invited Lizzie and Walt and Victor to come along on this trip. That was why John had cared so much about coming back here this summer. Why hadn't he told her what it meant to him, instead of just acting stubborn about it?

Rose cried out suddenly, "It's coming! I can't hold it!"

"Victor!" Serena called in terror.

Serena helped him, doing as he said, pouring the freshly boiled water, bringing towels, standing by Rose, holding her hand. She had no time to think of what she was doing.

"Now bear down hard," Victor said. "Get your breath; once more, now."

Serena bent close to Rose, whispering encouragement, "It'll be over in a few minutes, Rose. You're wonderful. Mike would be proud of you . . ." she, who knew nothing of childbirth.

Victor said nothing beyond his directions. He acted, Serena thought in her excitement, as though Rose were just some dispensary patient he had paid to get to come to the hospital. Serena fanned flies away with a newspaper, fanning more swiftly in her anger. She looked down to see Victor holding something in his hands.

"It's a quite well-formed boy." He spoke as if Rose weren't there.

"I want to see him." Rose sat up suddenly. "Is he . . . is he dead?"

"Of course it's dead, and it's too strange to look like a real baby to you," Victor said. He did not let her see the fetus, and carried it out to the kitchen. Rose lay back, burying her face in the pillow. She made no sound. Serena squeezed her hand and brushed back her hair. She fanned away the flies that buzzed noisily against the window by the bunk. Suddenly, she came back to Rose and stooping, kissed her head.

"Never mind, Rose; you lost it because you rode so hard to help Mike. You'll have another baby. . . ." Rose lay still, her face hidden in the pillow.

Serena went out to the lean-to kitchen for water to bathe Rose's face. Victor was placing the lid back on the stove. A sharp, stinging odor caught at her nose.

"What are you doing, Victor?"

Serena lifted the lid of the stove. The little dead fetus lay in the stove. Flames licked up around it. Serena looked at Victor. Her mind jumped back to yesterday when they had held the warm, live grouse between them. She had seemed so close to him. Now something dead lay between them. She couldn't speak.

"What's the matter? Would you rather have me bury it? I thought this was cleaner. I want to be cremated, myself."

"Take it out!" Serena said quietly. Her throat ached. Her eyes stung. Her mouth drew down painfully when she tried to speak. The flames rose above the opening of the stove. She watched one flame bend against his bare wrist as he reached in. The charred stench deepened. It was already burning.

"Sorry, I can't get it," Victor said. He put the lid back on the stove. Serena went out to the porch till the wave of sickness that washed up through her died down.

"I'm sorry," Victor said, coming back from caring for Rose. "I thought the sooner out of the way the better. You might try her with some tea again."

It was eleven o'clock. Rose was asleep. Serena had taken as long as she could to wash the few dishes and straighten the cabin. Finally she came back to sit on the porch.

"Is she sleeping?" Victor asked.

"Yes."

"This is a new experience for you."

"I suppose it is," Serena said slowly. She had not

thought of it as an experience; it was rather as though it were happening to her.

They sat still so long Serena had a queer sense of unreality. The light was hazy, saturated with smoke. The heat pressed on them like some pressure on the head. The sandy ground in front of the step looked hot, and the needles of the scraggly pine tree had lost their deep green. Beyond the reef, the sky was swollen and red to soreness. Heat still came from the door of the cabin, heat and death and suffering.

Victor handed her a cigarette and held a lighted match against it. She saw a red streak on his wrist.

"You burned yourself, didn't you?"

"It's nothing; burning is the order of the day."

She might say she was sorry, but she didn't.

"Serena, I'm sorry that bothered you. The sooner that girl forgets this episode the better, you know."

Serena stared into the dry, yellow-green shifting of the aspen leaves. "When you resigned because those other doctors had been dismissed, it wasn't because you cared about the men, themselves, was it?" she asked quietly, without looking at him.

"No, I don't suppose it was. If they'd been leaving of their own accord, going to some other university, I should have been glad to see some of them leave. Hoffmeyer was always a thorn in my flesh because of his preoccupation with the thymus gland."

Wednesday

"It was just—just the principle of the thing," Serena murmured in a cool tone John knew and hated, but its significance was lost on Victor.

"Yes, as much as anything. I never claimed to be a great lover of mankind, Serena. You made me that in your imagination and with your American sentimentality. I lay claim chiefly to being honest. I didn't care to live in a country where such unfair things could happen."

"I see," Serena said, going silently into the cabin.

12

"HE'S alive. He's just done in," Burns said.

Walt lay on the ground outside the mine shaft. Burns had felt some freshness creeping into the smoke-filled atmosphere of the cave and crawled, half fearfully, out past the fallen timbers at the entrance. The fire had swept on up the mountain, but the thick duff and burned logs still smoldered in the pale, half-light of early morning. Then he had roused Harley. Together, they had dragged Walt outside. The three men looked at the blackened woods as though looking at a strange world, dumbly. Walt breathed in the hot, parched air, noisily, as though he were afraid to stop breathing. Their eyes were bloodshot. Smoke, soot, singeing, had made them all curiously alike.

Burns looked at his boots and found them charred black. He touched the burn on his arm with wary fingers. It ran from his shoulder to his elbow, and his shirt and heavy woolen underwear were burned to the skin. Blisters stood out on his back like the blisters on a burned piece of painted wood.

"That was a close one!" the ranger said.

"Look at that!" Walt said weakly, his eyes on a fifty-foot spruce tree in front of him. It stood straight as a telegraph pole, stripped of every green needle; yet its trunk and each branch still glowed red.

"The darn thing looks like a human spine with all the nerves running out from it. We used to have to name the nerves. . . ." He laughed foolishly. Burns and Harley didn't laugh. Burns was looking at him with a puzzled expression. Then Walt remembered. He pulled himself up to a sitting position.

"Burns, didn't you find John?"

Burns was silent. The ranger shook his head. "If he didn't find some way to get out of there, he's dead. The mine shaft only just saved us."

"But there wasn't any way, was there?" Walt asked slowly in a low voice.

"You can't tell," the ranger answered. Burns still said nothing. He was trying to pull his boot on with his bandanna wrapped around his foot. Suddenly he dug up his own morsel of comfort and gave it to Walt, limp and useless from his mind's worrying.

"John knows this part of the woods. He was always tramping up here, fishing, in the summers. He might even know it better than I do." Then he added, "But I thought he might know about the mine shaft and find his way to it."

"Nobody could have got there any later than we did," Harley said.

"Last night, in that cave, I kept thinking I heard him yelling for help. I'd look out and think I saw him coming," Walt said.

"God, yes!" Burns muttered.

Harley wiped his face with a burned rag that had been a bandanna.

Walt rolled over on his side and got to his knees. He felt as limp as he had three years ago after that attack of pneumonia. Harley helped him to his feet. Walt took a long breath.

"I guess I'll sit down for a while," he said with a smile.

"You wait here while we go up the creek; I'd like to get you out of the glare . . ." Harley said.

Burns looked significantly around. No sprig of green was left, only black charred stumps of trees, ugly and misshapen. Ashes floated in the air, drifting against their faces, sticking to their lips. Walt licked his lips with his tongue and spit the clinging ash out, trying to be rid of the everlasting taste of smoke.

"O.K. You'll go on to find Mike?" Walt asked.

He was conscious of the miracle of speech again, hearing his words as he said them.

Harley nodded.

"What about John?"

"We'll keep a watch out for him, but he was lost back a way. We better go on up to Bear Creek first. Tell the first man that comes through here about John's being missing," Harley said.

"I used to tell the boy plenty of times what to do in a forest fire," Burns mumbled to himself. "I've told him there wasn't anything one man could do against a big fire if it got into the trees so it rode the tops. The only thing to do was to light out, and then I led him right into one."

"Nothing would have kept him from going for Mike, Burns," Walt said gently, as he had said to parents whose child had been brought in from a bicycle accident. "You mustn't blame yourself."

"I guess that's right. I never thought John was much like his old man, but he's just as softhearted," Burns said sadly.

"Sure you'll be all right?" Burns asked again as they left Walt, propped up against a charred stump with the burned remnant of Harley's jacket for a pillow and his canteen freshly filled from the slow trickle of water in the mine shaft.

"I'm fine. Good luck to you," Walt said heavily.

He watched them go stumbling through the windfall. "Lord, what a thing!" he said aloud. "Go off on a pack trip for the fun of it and end up with a . . . a mess like this!"

Burns and Harley were out of sight, and he sat alone in the waste of burned snags and smoldering duff. It was more desolate than the mountains of the moon. He tried closing his eyes to stop the smarting, but he didn't feel safe with them closed. He opened them again. Unaccountably, he was shivering.

Burns and Harley worked their way slowly across the windfall. Once Burns caught his leg between two charred logs and fell heavily. He pulled himself up in silence.

"I didn't hear you say anything," the ranger said grimly.

Burns made a sound, half a laugh, half a grunt. "Couldn't say anything strong enough."

The woods were so empty of sound their voices took on a thin, weird quality. "This looks like parts of the Argonne forest," Burns said, looking off through the desolate waste.

"Took a good many years to grow it, too," the ranger said. He felt beaten. This was the first fire to get away from him this summer. The end of last month he'd been congratulating himself. This was worse than the Hungry Man fire two years ago.

They came on the charred carcass of a buck, caught by a leg as he leaped through the windfall. They went around it without a word, but the thought in each man's mind was the same.

They could still see the fire sweeping up the mountain. The roar came faintly down to them, but they had no part in it. Burns didn't even look up. The wind was dying out some; ought to get it under control by night, but there wouldn't be much left by then.

A plane flew over them so close they could see the green paint on its wings. It went on in the direction of the fresh fire.

"They may have given us up for dead," Harley said.

"Would be, too, if it weren't for that damn mine shaft," Burns muttered.

Then they came to the stream, which was choked black with cinders. They knelt down beside it, pushing away the wood coals so they could drink, but the cinders drifted back against their mouths and hands. This water, too, was warm, flat, flavored with charcoal. A burned log lay across the creek, and they had to crawl under it to get by. Branches on the upper side of the log held up charred spikes.

Burns went first. "Creek's about dried up from here on. Smell that!" He stood upright beyond the log. Almost at his feet lay the burned carcass of a horse, so large it bridged the stream. Silver mountings on a piece of burned leather bridle were black as old tin and half melted.

"It's Pay Dirt, his rodeo horse," Harley said.

"Isn't hard to figger out, is it?" Burns moved on around the horse.

"We'll find the boy near here," Harley added. They talked more loudly than they needed in the dead stillness, saying unnecessary things, going ahead slowly, their eyes searching.

Mike's body was ashes; the black mound crumbled where they touched it. Only the shoes held their shape.

"When the fire hit here, it was sure traveling," the ranger said slowly.

Burns walked away, hunting out the place where Mike had had his tent. A black coffee pot lay on its side and a saw. He found the place where Mike had had his logs piled. Smoke and heat still rose from the huge pile of ashes.

"They figgered on enough logs for three rooms," Burns said aloud, but to himself. He came back to Mike's body. He turned something with his toe and stooped to pick it up. It was Mike's belt buckle. He held it in his hand. It was something to take to Rose. Then he let it drop to the ground. What good would that do Rose?

"He didn't get very far," Harley said.

"Nope," Burns said, "I think Mike would have got out; at least he wouldn't have been caught right here if he hadn't tried to get Pay Dirt out. He set a lot of store by that horse."

"Yes, I remember them at the Fair," Harley said.

"If we could have gotten through to him last night, d'you think we could have saved him?"

Harley shook his head. "I was afraid we couldn't when we started out, but it was worth a try. I think he was caught about the time the wind trapped us. If it hadn't been for that wind . . ."

Burns started to say something and stopped. Then he said it in spite of himself.

"We'll cut back over and find John like that."

Harley's face was sober. "You never know, Burns, till you find him."

A fitful gust of wind rose in the woods, blowing the smell of burned flesh against their faces, stirring the black ashes into a whirligig. Burns choked unexpectedly, and his eyes watered.

"John knew every inch of the stream. If he could have found it, he might have saved himself," he said.

"The stream isn't far from where the fire separated us," Harley said encouragingly, "but there's an awful steep cliff there."

Burns looked around the woods, at the ashes that had been Mike and at the half-burned body of the horse. Near the horse a little flame crept out, fanned to life by the fresh wind; low, harmless, without body, that would die down of itself. He saw it and stamped on it with a sudden blind rage, cursing as he stamped it out. Then he picked up the belt buckle for the second time and put it in his pocket.

"I don't know how that girl'll ever take this," he said to Harley. Then he wondered about Serena. She was different. She and John . . . she was a queer one for John.

It was harder going back. Their burns hurt. They stumbled through the windfall, falling over the black logs, getting up more wearily each time. Smoke like a whine rose into the air from every smoldering log.

"It's almost noon," Harley said.

"You'd never know it from the sun," Burns grunted.

They found Walt talking to a new crew of CCC boys coming in to relieve the others. Burns and Harley came up to them without any greeting. The CCC boys nodded, a queer expression, almost of embarrassment, on their faces. They had been told before they started out to look for the bodies of these three. It made them seem different from ordinary men to the boys.

Walt looked at Burns and Harley, and knew without asking that they had found Mike.

"I told them about John," Walt said. "One of them went right back to report to the head ranger."

"Yeah," a boy with red hair broke in. "The ranger'll have men all over here in no time. They'll pick him up if he's . . ." The boy stopped, embarrassed, as he recognized Harley. With his shirt hanging in burned shreds, his trousers blackened and torn to a colorless state, his hair and eyebrows singed, Harley hadn't looked like the ranger the boys all knew.

They started back, Walt between them. Gradually, men from the fire line on their way back to the camp overtook them. They were dog-tired, blackened with smoke, red-eyed, but joking. They called out to each other, telling how much they could eat, jostling, kidding. Then the word trickled back about Mike. One man murmured to another and glanced ahead at Burns or Walt or Harley, and a silence tinged with curiosity or awe fell on them all.

Walt wasn't prepared for the size of the fire camp

that filled the clearing. It was laid out like an army camp. They passed a radio operator sitting at a bench. Food was laid out on long serving tables. Over at one side of the camp, trucks were drawn up in two lines. Harley left them to report to Jackson. Burns and Walt went on their way back to their own camp. Burns was trying to think how he could best tell Rose.

Lizzie saw them, and came running. "Walt, are you all right? Burns, I'm so glad you're all safe. I've never spent such an awful day. But you're both such horrible messes!" she said, laughing with relief.

"Where's Rose?" Burns asked. ". . . and Serena?"

"Oh, Walt, Rose got back from that ride to tell someone about the fire, you know, and she began having terrible pains. When Victor came, he said she was having a miscarriage, and he and Serena took her to town in the truck. I waited here for you." Her words spilled out over each other.

Burns looked almost relieved. "You two go on into town in a truck. I'm going to get myself a new pair of boots, and then I'm going back to get John."

"John!" Lizzie cried out. "Why, where is John? And what about Mike?"

"Mike's dead, Lizzie," Walt said in a low voice. "And John's lost. Harley saved our lives by keeping us in an old mine shaft all night." A shudder went through him as he told it.

"Why, Walt!" Lizzie murmured incredulously. "How awful!"

"It was horrible. I don't see how John could be alive. Burns, don't go yet, better get rested. . . ."

Burns shook his head. "I've got to go back and find the boy. You go on into town. Jackson has had our horses looked after; I'll bring 'em later. You better tell Rose about Mike. Just tell Serena that John and I are still working in the woods."

"I'll get you something to eat, first," Lizzie said, her pretty face small and pinched with fear.

13

THE truck bumped and wrenched its way back across the rough flats to the town. Victor sat up with the driver. Rose lay on an air mattress and a sleeping bag on the floor of the truck. Serena sat at the end, her legs in blue jeans hung over the edge. She watched the faint wheel tracks curve and twist, a gopher springing up out of a hole with a sharp little squeak. Smoke hung low over the line of mountains they had seen so clearly going in. Dust blew up around the truck, and small pebbles scattered under the wheels. The air smelled as strongly of smoke here as back in the canyon. The prairie was ugly and weathered. Sagebrush and cactus and stones had become the same dun color. It was a terrible country, Serena thought, touching her lips that three days in the mountains had made rough and blistered.

She looked back into the hot darkness of the

truck. Rose lay still. That was better than having her whisper over and over again, as she had in the cabin, "I know he's dead or he'd be here." And then she would change and say, "He can't be dead. Mike would get out somehow. He'd ride. You ought to see Mike ride Pay Dirt."

Serena had lost so much sleep her eyes felt like crevices in the rocks. She wished John and Walt and Burns would come. She wasn't worrying, but they'd been gone a long time. Why didn't they come? It would be better for Rose to know. Her own mind had given up Mike, entirely.

The printing on the grain elevator was plain now: J. A. DAVIS. John's initials were J. A., too. It was queer to have your name—well, it was hers—standing out in a little prairie town like this, facing the mountains. John ought to see that they painted it off.

The truck swung into the main highway. The white line marking the middle of the hard black surface was just under her feet. She had never seen it at close range before or thought of it. It made her dizzy to watch it. There was the gasoline station they had passed on the way out. It was funny to see the town backward like this. She turned around to look through the front. Rose was sitting up, cross-legged on her mattress, powdering her nose.

"Why, Rose! How do you feel?"

"Like the stuffing was knocked out of me, but I don't want any of the town thinking I was sick. His folks might be down, and they don't even know I was going to have a baby yet, unless they just guessed it. I don't like his folks much. They thought I was that way when we got married, 'cause nobody ever tied Mike up before. But they were wrong. Mike married me because he loved me."

"Are you sure you ought to sit up?"

"Sure, I'm fine." Rose applied rouge from a puff and compact in the pocket of her jeans, but the bright color only made her pallor more striking.

The truck stopped in front of the forest service headquarters, and a knot of people around the doorway came toward it, staring curiously in at Rose and Serena.

"Hi, Rose!" someone said.

"Hi," Rose answered. She slid to the end of the truck and jumped off lightly. Then Serena saw her hold hard on to the edge of the truck. She put out her hand to help her, but Rose moved away from it.

"Hear you got burned out?" one of the men said.

"You hear a lot down here where you're safe, don't you, Jim!" Her eyes flashed.

"Well," Victor said. "You recovered!"

Serena pressed his arm. "Rose doesn't want anyone to know she's been sick," she murmured.

Victor nodded. "They'll drop us at the hotel as soon as he's finished reporting to the ranger there. I'll go in and see if they know anything more."

The crowd of townspeople pressed closer. It made Serena think, oddly, of a crowd in front of a summer theater in Connecticut, though the people were so different. They seemed to be waiting for something. They were mostly women and children; the men were fighting the fire in the woods. Serena lighted a cigarette and passed one to Rose. Carefully, she put out the match, tramping it into the dust in front of the ranger's office.

"Look at her, smoking as cool as though she didn't give a snap about him."

Serena looked up sharply. She glanced at Rose, but Rose hadn't heard. Rose was sitting on the truck, leaning against the side. Serena was uneasy. She felt a queer excitement in the crowd. A girl, Rose's age, came over to talk to them.

"Gosh, it's an awful fire, ain't it? Mike was pretty far in the woods, too." But she went no farther. Did she know anything about Mike? Serena studied the girl's bland face. Victor and the truck driver came out of the log house. Victor swung himself up on the edge of the truck beside them.

"We'll go up to the hotel and get a room where you can lie down," he said to Rose. "I think I'd be careful to rest a large part of the time for the next few days. Do your parents live here? Would you rather go right to them?" Serena noticed the kindness in his voice.

Rose shook her head. "The ranch is eighteen miles east o' here, and no one's there now. Pop got himself a job on the road when we didn't have no crop."

Serena caught Victor's eye. Something was wrong. Victor knew then; Mike was dead. He'd found out from the ranger.

She looked at the flimsy houses along the main street, at the beer halls and main store and post office that she had seen on their way in, but each one took on a certain terrible sharpness. In spite of herself, she read the signs on the front of the store: "Golden Plug Tobacco; Levi Overalls, made with copper rivets. . . ." It couldn't be; Mike couldn't be dead. She looked at Rose. Rose seemed to stare indifferently at the town.

As they went through the lobby of the hotel Serena felt people watching them curiously.

"Hi," was Rose's greeting to everyone.

The hotel clerk seemed to look at them with sorrowful eyes. "Worst fire this country's ever seen! Yes, sir, 's the worst fire this side o' the divide. We've got three truckloads of men in the dining room now filling up before they take 'em into the mountains; shipped 'em here from all over."

"They need them," Victor said, signing the register.

"Well, it'll give 'em work for a few days. They say the man that started the fire was out o' work an' wanted fire-fighting pay."

"We'll take three rooms. . . ."

"No, Rose and I will be together," Serena said quickly.

They went up the shabby stairs. The rooms were clean enough, but the low ceilings made them seem twice as small. Rose dropped wearily on the bed.

"I sure tucker out easy."

Serena followed Victor outside into the hall. "Vic, you heard. . . ."

"He was burned to death," Victor answered softly. "I think you better tell her."

"Oh, Victor, I couldn't. I wouldn't know how to do it. Couldn't we wait till Burns and John come?"

"I'm afraid she'd hear the people talking about it; I was fearful of that at the ranger's station. How about a drink first?"

"No, I'll go in and tell her first," Serena said slowly.

Victor looked in at the dingy "cocktail parlor" at the left of the hotel desk, but it was so near noon that it was quite deserted. He went on down the street until he came to the corner drugstore. This was the real gathering place for the town. The stools in front of the pink marble fountain were full. People came here to buy papers and talk about the fire. He heard snatches of their conversation and caught their covert glances of curiosity directed toward him. The radio blared tirelessly back of the fountain.

He ordered a Coca-Cola and wondered if the girls would be shocked if he took them something to drink, if he would seem insensitive to Serena. It was hard to tell. She had been so upset at the cabin over his burning the fetus; he had had no idea that it would bother her. She was shocked, too, over his coming back from the fire, but it was a fortunate circumstance for Rose. He smiled thinking about Serena trying to handle the delivery by herself. She was amazingly ignorant of so many things. He felt that she had turned completely away from him, back to her husband, finding him a hero. Well, that was pleasant if her husband could manage to retain his heroic stature in her eyes.

Two days ago, he had felt so at ease with these Americans; now he found himself entirely separated. He finished his glass. What a horrible drink Coca-Cola was!

He had picked up the mail at the hotel and brought it along without sorting it. The two for himself told him what he feared without opening them. He laid them out on the table in front of his glass. They were addressed in his own handwriting to Fräulein Kathie Huber. Written across the corner were the words "Not at this address, try . . ." Four such addresses had been tried, and finally, stamped in red ink over them all, the significant "Not known."

Kathie had helped one too many escape out of Vienna and had been found out.

He sat looking at the envelope without opening it. He had no desire to read his own words, his explanations; call it his apologia. He had been perfectly right not to stay. If he had not left Austria, he could only have helped others for a short time before he would have been caught like Kathie. Oh, he was perfectly right to get out when he did, but, nevertheless, he would not have lost Kathie, not in the same way.

Unless the Wind Turns

He looked out the window, past the new display of hot-water bottles and bathing caps, on to the main street of Sweet Springs, Montana. Above the letters on the glass, the ugly grain elevator was visible, and the faded letters J. A. DAVIS. John Davis and Kathie—were they not a little alike?—he thought as his eyes came back unhappily to the envelopes.

14

ROSE was lying with her face buried in the pillow when Serena came back into the room. Serena was seized with a kind of panic at being here alone with her. Maybe she was asleep. She went over to the wash basin and drew some water.

She heard Rose move on the bed. "You can't even begin to get the grime off with this cold water," she said experimentally, without looking up. Rose made no answer. When Serena turned around, she was lying on her back, staring out the window of the bedroom. Tears rolled down her face, and her mouth was oddly distorted.

"Rose . . . Rose, dear," Serena said haltingly. She had to make herself cross the room and sit down on the bed. She was torn with pity at the sight of her, but repulsed, too.

"I know," Rose said thickly. "He's dead. I knew right away at the ranger's station; the way folks looked at me."

The terrible little room closed in around them. Serena had nothing ready to say. She couldn't bring herself to touch her. She wanted only to get out of here, off by herself. This was the way she felt sometimes when John loved her, bearing down on her with his body and mind, and she could hardly wait to be free.

Then she was ashamed at being so busy with her own feelings. She twisted her hands together hard, knotting the bones of her knuckles together. She felt as though they had been sitting like this for a long time. She must say something, put her arm around Rose. . . . It had been so easy back there in the cabin . . . that was different.

"Rose, dear . . ."

Rose sat up in bed. "I don't see how it could be Mike. Maybe folks just think he was trapped in there, and all the time he's safe somewheres."

Serena's mind clutched at her hope. Let her hope as long as she could. Let Victor tell her later. When John came back he could tell her. No, she must tell Rose. It was cowardly and cruel to let her hope.

"Rose, it's true. They know for sure. Burns found his body. When Victor went into the station, the ranger told him." Her words came out bluntly, in short, bold sentences that stood alone, hanging in the air, where they went on sounding like a note struck by a tuning fork. The sound of them ran together, so it didn't seem like her voice. She was looking at Rose. Rose's lips quivered, but she didn't cry. Her eyes clung to Serena's.

"Where did Burns find his body? Why couldn't he get out?"

"I don't know, Rose. Victor'll tell you all he knows. Lizzie will bring Burns and John and Walt in as soon as they come."

This was the time when people told other people to be brave. How could they? She couldn't tell that to Rose. She wished she would cry again. Rose sat so still. A car started out in the street. Serena had almost forgotten there was any life outside these four walls. Someone ran up the wooden stairs. Serena hoped for a moment that it might be John, but the steps went by their room to a room down the hall. A door banged so that the picture on the wall slid down crookedly at one corner. The person in the next room turned on a radio, and they heard it crackling. Serena started up from the bed.

"I'll tell them to turn it off," she said indignantly. But before she had crossed to the door, the words she heard stopped her.

". . . Mike Logan, twenty, logging in the vicinity of Bear Creek was found burned to death. Close by was the body of his horse, Pay Dirt. It is thought Logan must have been trying to lead his horse out of the timber when the fire overtook him. The party of four men, headed by Ranger Harley, was trapped. Three of them found refuge all night in the entrance to an old mine shaft. One of the party, John Davis, became separated from the others. No trace of him has yet been found. It is feared that he may have perished on his way to rescue Logan. Davis is the son of J. A. Davis, former . . ."

Serena sat down on the bed, hearing no more of the voice that came through the thin walls. Out of long habit, her hand felt of her hair, cupping the soft roll in her neck, pressing the hair between her fingers where it waved back from her forehead. Her eyes met Rose's. This couldn't be. John didn't even belong here. He had just come back of his own free will, because he loved the mountains. He couldn't be burned to death out on a pack trip like that.

She looked around the room mechanically, at the blotchy blue calcimine, at the white curtains that were uneven along the hem, at the dresser with the soiled blue pincushion and the Gideon Bible. They were all real. These things had been here when they came into town two days ago, waiting for her to come and sit in this room and hear about John. All her life she had wanted to be free of places, free to go away if a place was unpleasant. Now it seemed as though all her life her restless movement had only led her to this place and this moment. Now she was caught.

She felt Rose's hand on hers as it lay on the bed and pulled her own away quickly. It tied her here. She and Rose in this hideous, hot little room.

"Gosh! He was the one that asked me to go with you. I thought he was the nicest of the bunch," Rose said. "Burns said he had made a real mountain man out of him, too."

Serena couldn't speak. She had only a desire to get away. She went over to the window and looked down on the street. From here she could see over the sham front of the beer hall opposite on to the flat tin roof that was really only one story high. She couldn't get her mind back to John yet. She couldn't make him real.

Burning. . . . She drove her mind back to the stove in John's cabin, the flames licking up out of the opening, the smell of burned flesh. She tried to keep her mind on these things. Really, she was thinking how she would have to stay here in this town, sleeping in this room tonight, waiting for them to bring his body out. People would look at her as they had at Rose, each having a claim on her because John came from here, because of her sorrow. This dreadful place and the mountains would always have a hold on her, no matter where she went.

Rose put her arm around her. Serena stood stiffly, but without drawing away. This girl whom she had never seen a week ago, this girl with her cheap perfume still clinging to her skin and her scraggly hair, stood between her and the hideous loneliness of this room.

"You've been taking care of me and trying to comfort me . . . you've been swell to me," Rose was saying.

Serena thought how easy it had been. She had thought she felt deeply with Rose, but all the time she had been separate and free and safe from feeling too deeply. She could see now.

"I know how you feel," Rose said. "You don't believe it, really. I guess I won't ever think of Mike as dead."

After a while, Rose said, "Anyway, we were married to our men. My folks wanted me to wait till next year. Gosh, I'm glad I didn't."

"We were married, but John and I . . . we; you see, you and Mike were different. Mike felt you loved him." There was no reason why she should tell all this to Rose, but some sense of honesty in her pushed the words out of her.

"I'll say he did. I've always loved Mike, but he

took his time getting that way about me," Rose said, almost smiling.

"And you were going to have a child for him."

"It wasn't for him so much," Rose said thoughtfully. "He didn't care whether we had a kid right off or not. I wanted the baby. A man's more settled with a kid of his own. If it hadn't been for that kid, Mike wouldn'ta decided to build a cabin this fall. He wouldn'ta got burned." She burst out crying.

"You mustn't think that way," Serena said. "You can't go back and think that if you hadn't done this something might not have happened."

If we had only gone to the Cape this summer, Serena thought; if I'd come out here alone with John. . . . She sat down on the armchair wearily. She had to go back, herself. It was all right to say you mustn't, but you couldn't help it.

Only two days ago she had stepped off the train. She went back to the first night in the mountains; John's wanting to love her and then not wanting to, almost as though she had failed him. But just before, he had said that about the others, "I don't care if they are along. You're here." And then the next day at the cabin he had said that about their marriage not meaning enough. Why didn't it?

If she hadn't invited Walt and Lizzie and Victor to come on this trip with them, if, instead, they had been alone together in his funny little shack, the way John had planned, what would it have been like? Would he have found what he seemed to find lacking in her? Would she have found something in John she hadn't known before, and never would now that he was gone? She was unaware that her eyes were wet.

"I was wrong when I said that about the kid." Rose's voice startled her. "I wish I could have kept it. He would have been something left of Mike for me to have."

Serena was silent. Almost shyly she looked at Rose, so tired and homely from crying, and envied her. She had never thought of having a child for that reason, because it would be part of . . . part of John.

Then Rose saw the tears in Serena's eyes. "You don't know he's dead for sure," she told her. "You don't want to give up hoping till you know."

"No, I don't know yet for sure," Serena repeated after her. A terrible eagerness filled her. She felt almost guilty with Rose, who knew for sure. "But that was what they said about Mike in the beginning," she said, hiding her hope.

15

JOHN had made his way from one log to another, creeping on his belly, for what seemed like hours. What if he were going in the wrong direction . . . away from the cliff?

He lay still, trying to get his breath, but the heat was so intense he couldn't endure it. He felt he was slowly roasting.

A spasm of anger filled him, and he lifted himself a little off the ground and lunged forward again. He strained until his chest ached to bursting and his eyes hurt so he was blinded. The effort exhausted him; couldn't keep this up any longer. He reached ahead with his arms. His hands were so badly burned they felt numb. He hardly knew what they touched, dirt or burning duff or . . . this time it was rock . . . so hot that he felt the heat through his numbness.

He lifted his head like a turtle, covering it with the jacket, trying to tie the sleeves together so it would stay. He hitched ahead again, groaning as he moved. The rock fell off abruptly, he could feel that much. This must be the cliff edge, then! He dropped his head, gasping for breath. He must shove himself over the edge; that was better than burning. He tried to hold on to the rock with his swollen hands, to pull himself forward with his arms, but the roar of the fire so close to him seemed to take the strength from him. A falling limb covered him with live sparks that burned where they touched.

He lunged forward desperately; he felt himself falling, and reached out frantic arms, suddenly strong again, to catch hold of something, anything.

He turned over as he rolled; loose scree rolled with him, then a snag raked his blistered arm. He grabbed hold, expecting it to break off in his grasp and let him fall.

Instead he came to a stop, the trunk of the snag holding him on the narrow ledge of rock that jutted out from the bank. His head pounded so he could only lie still, suspended above the gorge.

Then he lifted his head, hardly daring to move his weight, and felt with his hand. The ledge ran back into a crevice. Carefully, he edged his body into the crevice until he was shielded from the worst of the burning heat.

He dug deep into the crevice with his fingers, and a chunk of soft moss came away. It was still green, unshriveled by the fire. He laid it against his eyes, one at a time, passing it gratefully down over his burned face. He laid it against his blistered lips and opened his mouth and licked it, trying to get some moisture from it. Painfully, he felt of his jeans. They were hot and ragged from burns; his left leg was burned more than the right, but rolling over the bank had pounded out the smoldering fire in his clothing. He was safe if he lay still without moving. Slowly, he turned over on his stomach and closed his eyes against the rock.

He must have slept. He found himself staring up at a murky sky above the top of the opposite canyon wall. Smoke hid the sun, but it was daylight. He could see no free fire. The roar was gone. He didn't move. His whole body ached, and he was conscious of being cold. He tried to take a deep breath, and stopped midway because of the pain in his chest. The effort left him panting and weak. He touched his lips and his tongue, and the lips felt swollen out of shape. His tongue was dry. He had used the last drop in his canteen; there was nothing for it. After a long time, he tried to make a sound, to call "Burns!" But the voice wasn't his; it made only a small noise, which made the place more empty.

Good old Burns—if he hadn't taught him all he knew, he would never have known enough to crawl on the ground and shelter by a log; he would never have reached this ledge.

What about Walt and Burns and Harley? What about Mike? Unless they had found their way to this bank and found a place to hang on, they were dead. The stillness was so heavy he felt sure they were not alive. He tried to call again, but his throat was too dry. The fire must have swept up this gorge and be up higher now, in the timber above Bear Creek. The firefighters would be up there.

He tried to spread his jacket around his shoulders. The thick leather was dry and cracked by the fire, but it had helped to save his life.

He tried to look down, but the height or the pain of his blistered body made him dizzy. He lay back again and closed his eyes. When his head stopped pounding, he began to think, slowly, as though making an effort not to move his body with his thinking. He went back to the beginning.

They had come on a pack trip two days ago. It had all been because of him. He had wanted to come. He had wanted to bring Serena. He had had some kind of a cockeyed idea that Serena and he could get together out here. Then Serena had dragged the others along, and he had asked Rose. It was pretty funny when you stopped to think about it, pretty darn funny and grim at the same time. Better let it go at that.

They'd been going ahead with the woods green and safe ahead of them, yesterday. His mind mocked at him, remembering how it had been yesterday . . . the sun slanting through the trees, pine needles fringing the shadows, the air steeped in the smell of pine and the green firs going on forever up the trail, as far as you could see. Walt had groused about the beauty growing monotonous!

They had walked right up to the fire, stepped right into it. It was low down, easy to put out, only they hadn't quite got it out. They had started after Mike Logan, then the wind had changed. The next thing they knew the fire was flying through the air, springing with a hideous roar to the tops of the trees, coming behind them faster than they could run. One minute Burns and Harley and Walt had been there, shouting to him, and the next instant they were gone, swallowed up in the smoke and fire.

Well, Victor had been right. They hadn't saved Mike, and maybe the others were dead. But they couldn't have known that the wind would turn.

Even Harley and Burns couldn't know that. They had to try, anyway. That was only decent. You couldn't know a man was in danger and not try to help. It was like all the arguments in favor of going to war. The arguments were true, "true and righteous altogether." The phrase slid into his mind; it belonged to something he had learned somewhere.

And if you got burned to death in the fire, you might be a hero. Only it wasn't quite like that. Once you got in it you were scared to death. Not about Mike; you forgot all about him in your fear for your own life. You ended by fighting for your own survival, so you weren't heroic after all; maybe no one was in war either.

Maybe Victor had seen that in Europe. Maybe there were plenty over there who knew that they fought for their own skins and no one else's. When he saw Victor, he'd tell him he saw his point. Maybe, he'd been a little smug and self-righteous about Victor. Victor's world had burned up; it was all burned over timber and smoldering duff. Maybe that made a difference in the way you looked at things.

He wondered if Serena were worrying about him. Of course, she thought he was dead. Serena would be moved because she thought him a hero; must watch out for that. He didn't want Serena's admiration. She was probably indignant at Victor even, if he knew Serena. He and Serena were pretty well washed up, as far as he could see. It was a good thing that he wasn't burned to death, so she wouldn't be torn by his heroic memory.

He shook himself out of his curious lethargy and crawled nearer to the edge of the rocky ledge. He saw he couldn't make it that way. He'd have to climb up. He leaned against the charred tree for support. Then his thoughts could stave off his need no longer. All he wanted in this world was water.

16

A TRUCK brought Walt and Lizzie into Sweet
Springs late in the afternoon. They had waited in
the hope of hearing something from Burns. After
supper, they all sat in the dismal lobby of the hotel,
close to the window, shielded from the front door
and the desk by the sprawling rubber plants. Lizzie's radio was by her chair, turned low, so that at
the first sound of any fire news she could turn it up.
Rose had just left with Mike's family.

"They wanted her to be there when Mike's
body was brought in," Serena said. "Isn't that
pathetic?"

"My God!" Walt exclaimed, thinking of the belt
buckle in Burns' pocket, but he said no more because of Serena.

"She seemed more cheerful, somehow," Serena
said wonderingly.

"She's the honored member of his family now, as

Mike's widow," Victor said. "I've seen that happen before. People are awed into respect by grief."

Serena looked at him without lifting her chin from her hand. "Are you always cynical, Victor?"

"I'm not cynical, Serena. The same strings don't pull all the puppets, that's all." His eyes rested on hers. She was a curious girl. He wondered what this would do to her.

"Walt, honestly you ought to go to bed," Lizzie said again, as she had been saying ever since they got in. "We'll come up and tell you the minute we know anything."

"Walt shook his head. "I'll wait till Burns comes back."

"Cigarette?" Victor asked him.

"No, thanks." Then he said wryly, "Too much smoke for a while."

"I don't see how John could be going along right with you and then all of a sudden not be there," Serena said.

"You can't imagine what it was like. Suddenly, you couldn't see a foot ahead of you, S'rena," Walt explained.

"It stays light a long time out here. That ought to help Burns," Lizzie said.

The whole town was on the street, leaning against the store windows, sitting in their cars, going to the

225

movies . . . waiting. Cars and trucks roared by on their way through. People from Piegan City drove out to see the fire. "It's a sight worth seeing against the mountains," people said. The forest service trucks had a special sound, a heavier sound, as they rumbled by, and the tired, bleary-eyed men in them were quiet as they drove along the street.

The hotel proprietor left his desk to go out and talk a while on the street. People asked about Rose and the party of dudes. They shook their heads in sympathy. The proprietor was a person of importance. When he came back in, he stopped a moment.

"They say they've got it pretty well licked, and it looks like rain, too. That's what it'll take to finish it up."

"Good," Victor said. He appreciated the hotel-keeper's urge to talk to them.

"I'd like to see it rain in those woods," Walt said slowly. "They're a mess."

"I'm going upstairs a few minutes. I'll be right down," Serena said.

"I'll go with you," Lizzie offered quickly.

"No, you stay with Walt." Serena ran up the stairs, her jodhpur boots clicking against the brass bands on the treads. She couldn't stand it down there. She couldn't stand sitting across from Victor. She hated him. He sat there so calmly, looking at her as though he understood her in some special way, analyzing her as he had Rose.

She shut the flimsy door of the room and lay on the bed that was still wrinkled from Rose's lying there. This room she had wanted to get away from this afternoon was a refuge. She wished Rose were here.

She wished Burns would come. Burns hadn't given up hope, or he'd be here. Nobody knew John as well as Burns. She wanted to talk to him. She wanted John. Her arms tightened around the thin pillow, and she buried her face in it. She lay that way a long moment; then she sat up, beating her fist against it in a futile, hopeless burst of rage.

She went over to sit by the window again, looking down on the street, waiting. She heard the rain start, a thin, scanty spatter against the screen. What good was the rain now?

The people walked up and down the street without minding the rain. "I hope it turns in and pours," one man said to another below her window.

"Too bad it didn't come twenty-four hours sooner," another voice answered.

The rain hurried the dusk, and the electric sign at the Texaco station and the neon sign over the beer hall sprang into light. The sign over the hotel made a red and blue pattern on the wet roof of the porch below Serena's window.

A truck was coming now. She heard it on the street. She leaned out against the screen to listen. She heard someone shout far down the street. The town made a holiday out of a fire, she thought angrily. The truck was slowing down; it was stopping in front of the ranger's station.

Now it was starting again. It was coming down the street . . . she could see it. Someone yelled. It sounded like a cheer. The truck was stopping in front of the hotel.

The front door of the hotel banged. Someone laughed; someone said "Burns."

Serena ran down the stairs of the hotel, through the lobby. Then she heard Lizzie calling her.

"John!" Her voice was shrill. It broke queerly.

"Here I am, Serena! I can stand, Burns." John's voice was hoarse. He laughed a little shakily. She had hold of his arm, helping him into the hotel.

"Look at you, John!" The burns on his face were angry blisters; he was hardly recognizable, a burned smell clung to him.

"Look at me! Look at Burns!" John laughed. Then he saw Victor. "We certainly didn't do any good, Victor; you were right."

Serena didn't hear what Victor said; she had gone

ahead to open the door. Burns and Victor helped John upstairs.

"In here, Burns," Serena said.

"We'd have left him at my place, Serena," Burns said, "but we knew you'd be worried. He was going to hole in there till he got in a little better shape, except for that."

Serena didn't answer. She was busy pulling the spread down off the bed, straightening the pillow, but she had heard. John had wanted to "hole in" there.

"You've got some bad burns. I'll see what I can scare up in the way of dressings and come right back. I'm doing general medicine these days," Victor said.

Serena fussed with the window shades, trying to make them hang straight, as though she were at home.

"You're lucky to be here, boy," Burns said. "We all are."

She noticed how tired Burns was. The weariness stood out under the soot and dirt. The three days had made him look years older. She could see how much he cared for John.

"Well . . ." Burns started to go. "Don't let him get up and head back for the mountains."

"I won't," Serena said, still not quite looking at John. "Thank you, Burns."

"Don't thank me. I shouldn'ta let him go in in the first place. Thank the boy for keeping his head. How he kept alive is still a miracle to me," Burns said.

She touched his arm. "You'll get some rest yourself, won't you? Why don't you stay here in the hotel?"

Burns leaned against the door jamb. "How's Rose?"

"She's wonderful," Serena said. "She lost her baby. Victor took care of her, and then we brought her back here and she heard about Mike."

Burns nodded.

"She's gone home with his family."

Burns sucked in his cheek. Then he shook his head again. "Well, good night."

The flimsy door was so thin it shook when he closed it. Burns' feet sounded tired.

Serena stood at the foot of the bed looking at John.

"It certainly was a swell pack trip!" John said. His voice startled her. His face was so blackened it obscured his expression. His eyebrows and the hair along the front were singed.

"It wasn't anything anyone could help," she said.

She felt ill at ease with him, but that didn't matter; he was here.

"Let me help you out of your clothes, John. Walt and Lizzie brought our packs in. You can even put on your own pajamas." She brought them and sat on the bed undoing his boots, not really looking at him.

"The soles of your boots are burned clear through!"

He grunted. She pulled them off gently. He let her take off the burned shirt.

"Say so if it hurts you too much."

He knew she would be this way, doing everything for him. She helped him on with his pajamas. Even the sheet hurt against his back and legs.

She tried to wash his face, but it hurt too much.

"Just let it be dirty," he muttered.

"I'm sorry," Serena said. She stood again at the foot of the bed. There was so much to tell him: about Rose, about the cabin and reading his journal and about Victor, but she couldn't think how to start.

"You were brave to go in for Mike," she said finally.

He made an unpleasant, mocking sound in his throat. He might have known Serena would be like this; Serena admired bravery, or what she thought was bravery.

"You notice we didn't get him out, don't you?" His voice was rough.

"I know, but that isn't it. Victor . . ."

He sat up in bed in spite of his burns. "Hell, Serena, don't be a fool. Victor had some sense; the rest of us didn't." He sank back on the pillow, exhausted by his outburst. He closed his eyes, they burned so. He wished Serena would go and leave him alone.

Serena reached up and turned off the naked electric-light bulb and raised the shades. The neon sign across the street threw a red light in the room.

"It was a good thing Victor came back because of Rose. She had a miscarriage, John. I guess you didn't know about it. She took word to the fire-guard, and when she got back she began to have pains. Victor and I took her back to your cabin and took care of her there."

"Tough!" he said after a long time.

"Oh, John, it was terrible, and then we came back to town and she heard about Mike. I started to tell her, but she had guessed."

He tried to think of Serena up here alone with Rose, tried to think how she would be. Or at his cabin; she must have hated that.

Wednesday

"And then while I was trying to say something to comfort her a little, we heard the radio in the next room telling about it. It said you had been lost."

"That was dramatic," he muttered, wondering how it must really have been. He didn't want her being fond of him now just because she couldn't stand the thought of his being almost burned to death or because she felt that he'd been heroic.

"I'd felt so sorry for Rose I could hardly stand it, John, but after I heard about you I knew I didn't really have the faintest idea how she'd felt until then."

They were strangely quiet until Victor came back. She turned on the light and fastened a newspaper around it. Victor began spraying John's burns.

"Now this may hurt—"

". . . 'just a little'!" John finished for him. "Why don't you get some real perfume while you're at it; I could use some in my present state." He kept up a series of wisecracks, but he was thinking hard about what Serena had said. "Thanks, Victor, that feels better; but it makes my hide feel like a crocodile's," he said when Victor had finished.

"You've got a fever. Of course, you would have with such a big area of burns," Victor told him. "You better stay right here for a few days."

"I'll be all right on the train. I thought we better

get out of here tomorrow. I guess everyone's had enough of the mountains."

"Well, it has been an experience!" Victor said with a laugh.

John glanced at Serena. She was so quiet. She was holding it against Victor that he'd left the fire; how tiresome that was of her.

"You don't need to wait here with me, Serena," he said when Victor had gone. "You look as though you could use some more sleep."

Serena sat over by the window. The thing must have hit her pretty hard, he thought.

"I want to stay," she said.

He thought about that. Then he shifted carefully against the pillow. "Listen, Serena, just because I was in danger don't feel you have to try to make it up to me. All this hasn't really changed anything."

"It's changed a lot of things," she said stubbornly. "We are going to stay right in Sweet Springs until you feel all right. The others can leave; I think they want to. You haven't had a chance to see the mountains or Burns, hardly." She was silent a minute; then she went on, avoiding his eyes. "It isn't burned around your cabin; we could go up there for a week or so after you're better."

234

Wednesday

He didn't get it. He didn't answer, trying to understand her.

Serena looked down the street of the town. Even in the rain, the dark bulk of the grain elevator seemed to shield the town. The mountains were lost out there somewhere. Across from the hotel, people were going into the movie as though there had been no fire. The town looked familiar, as though she had known it for a long time.

"I'll go down and tell them all that we've decided to stay on. I imagine they're anxious to make their train reservations. I'll be right back."

He listened to her footsteps on the stairs. An uncertain smile hurt his stiff face. She hadn't even waited for him to agree, he thought. That was Serena for you!